Bad Day in Greenville

Joe Flint got up that morning to just another day in Greenville. But when you live in a border town in New Mexico every day is different: this was going to be a bad one. Who was the dead man on the mysterious coach that rode into town? A coach that carried a badly injured woman and a crying child. Who was the drifter called Ty who came into town and who wanted to find out about the injured woman?

When Flint tries to investigate the mystery merely deepens. He has to go to the nearby prosperous town of Afton and find out if anyone there knows who the girl and the dead man are. The investigation should be simple enough, yet he is soon dragged into a fight for his own life. But with the help of a stranger Flint learns to fight back against the evil Nat Parker for the answers he so richly deserves.

Bad Day in Greenville

Alex Frew

A Black Horse Western

ROBERT HALE

ISBN 978-0-7198-2248-3

The Crowood Press
The Stable Block
Crowood Lane
Ramsbury
Marlborough
Wiltshire SN8 2HR

www.bhwesterns.com

Robert Hale is an imprint
of The Crowood Press

Typeset by
Derek Doyle & Associates, Shaw Heath
Printed and bound in Great Britain by
CPI Group (UK) Ltd, Croydon, CR0 4YY

CHAPTER ONE

Greenville was in Doña Ana county, New Mexico, not too many miles from El Paso to the east, and from the border of the adjoining state of Texas. It was a town of expansion and contradiction. The area had been inhabited for thousands of years by the Pueblo Indians, and even though the days of the Mexican Indian Wars seemed all but gone, Greenville still had memories of a short but violent past to dwell on. The territory was still considered to be theirs by many Mexicans, and not just the low-born *campesinos*, either, but the more nobly born who remembered the days when they were ruled by the Hapsburg empire. It was common to see Mexicans on the streets and in the saloons conducting business and many of the buildings of the town had a distinctly Spanish feel about them.

Thanks to the Homestead Act (generally regarded by the local inhabitants as a Land-grabbing Act) the area was nominally owned and ruled by white American settlers.

Joe Flint was thinking of some of those anomalies as he took a slow swagger around the town. It was getting towards eleven and like most inhabitants he wanted to be finished in enough time to indulge in his mid-day siesta. In his experience the sheriffs in most of these small border towns were individuals who avoided as much work as they could, drank a great deal of coffee, stayed indoors warmed by their pot-bellied stoves, and leaned heavily on their deputies to actually get any work done. This was not his style.

When he took a job he made sure it was done properly. He patrolled the town morning and night. He listened to the gossip in the saloons and coffee-houses, and he watched out for what was going on. That way he was often able to nip trouble in the bud before it had time to blossom. Trouble was never that far away in a town like this, where tensions could rise high between the many cattle-dealers, farmers, and people of a distinctly shady character who passed through any border town, and who could leave a trail of destruction in their wake.

His thoughts turned then to Afton, the nearest town, about twelve miles away as the crow flew and quite a bit more by the rutted trails that passed for roads in these parts. Despite being situated only a short distance back from the border Afton had every-thing that Greenville lacked. It had been built on the success of the Santa Fe cattle trail, the coming of the South-Western railways, and on mining silver, none of which showed any signs of ceasing to be profitable in this year of 1881. Afton's streets were wide and the place had a solid, prosperous air: the main drag was one of several tree-lined boulevards, and there were redstone townhouses for the rich who still lived there and hadn't decamped back North to live the high life in New York or stand for Congress in Washington.

Flint envied Ben Couhard, the sheriff of that town. They weren't buddies in any shape or form, but they had met for the occasional beer when business of one kind or another brought them together. Ben was a little older, a little slower and gave the impression that he did as he was asked by the authorities, albeit with his deputies doing most of the work. Without actually saying a single derogatory word he managed to make Flint feel like a country cousin.

The town of Afton had some local characters like Douglas Quinn; a man who had made a fortune on railway stock, rightly sensing that a large number of people were willing to bet on the railways. By taking their investments and putting them into rail for commission, he had made far more money than anyone who invested in the railways directly. He was also the owner of several hardware stores and a business that offered loans to the unwary on the High Street in Afton. He was rich beyond the dreams of Flint, who accurately described himself as 'just an ordinary Joe'. Yet they said that Quinn, for all his money, was lonely and reclusive, that he had retired to his timber-framed mansion on the edge of town after disastrous relationships with his family.

Joe didn't know most of the details; he was entirely

7

uninterested in the lives of rich men. He was more worried about the outlaws who crossed the borders around here. Greenville was set between the Doña Ana mountains, the flood plains of the Rio Grande, and the southern end of the San Andres mountains, and it was easier to cross the border here than go by the hills.

In his office he had a pile of papers and posters relating to fugitives from the law: Norales, Gonzales, the Clancy brothers Jack and Dave, Gil Beemis, 'Hot' Hodges, and even one or two women like Rural Annie and Bad Liz.

Most of the posters for these criminals were of little or no help. The one of Beemis had him looking rather like a gorilla, at least going by illustrations of those beasts that Flint had seen in some of the more sensational dime adventure stories that he liked so much to read, while Bad Liz looked as if she had even more muscles than Flint, who was in good condition and still in his thirties. Today he was wearing a blue shirt that had faded a little with time, but it fitted well and was one of his favourites.

His mind turned from outlaws to a more pressing subject, that of his 'friend' Katie-Jo. He thought back to how he had met her. As the local sheriff in a town of about a thousand inhabitants, some of his more pleasurable tasks were to go to local events such as the horse races that the cowboys held during the day at the weekends, or the social events hosted by the richer inhabitants.

There was also a local dance held at least once a

month on a Saturday in the schoolhouse, a big dark-brown wooden building in the middle of town that had been paid for by public taxes and some private philanthropy. The schoolhouse had two classrooms, one for the small children and one for those over eight years old. Most children went to school only until they were twelve.

When a dance was to be held the desks and chairs would be stacked against the green-painted walls, then in would troop men who were cowboys and sod-busters by day, bearing fiddles, guitars, squeezeboxes and drums. They would form an ad hoc band, playing a mixture of old Irish and Scottish tunes, or Spanish airs played with great gusto, along with folk-songs and waltzes from the rest of Europe and from America itself, the songs of Stephen Foster such as 'Camptown Races,' and 'Oh Susannah!' being particularly popular.

Joe was usually content to stand with a beer and chat with the other men, not making any particular effort to join in the merriment, but one day his eye was caught by a particularly fine-looking young lady in her early twenties who, like the other women who attended, was using the dance as an excuse to dress in her finest clothes. She wore a black dress, a red silk scarf and red dancing shoes. Her shining fair hair was held back from her face by a band of patterned ivory and she had the most sparkling eyes and perfect bowed lips he had ever seen.

'Who's that girl?' he asked the mayor, a whiskery old man of sixty called Oscar Chavez, who was a seed merchant in his working life.

'A pretty sight, as you can see,' said the mayor. 'That's Katie-Jo Landers, the new schoolma'am. Hired her myself, Señor Flint – well, me with the other members of the eddication board.'

'I thought the school was supervised by Miss Morse.' Flint pictured the rather thin, serious spinster in his mind.

'Surely is, but the population's only gettin' bigger,' said Chavez. 'Soon be gettin' more pupils and we need an educated set o' kids who can read and write in these modern times.'

'Sure,' said Joe sturdily. He himself had not had much of an education, yet he loved books and was self-taught in all the important matters of his life. Still, he was quite startled when the young lady in question lighted upon him and gave him an arch glance from under those shapely eyebrows.

'Sheriff Flint,' she said, in a tone that seemed to mock and approve of him at the same time. 'Care to dance with the new girl?'

He was not a dancer but some impulse moved him forward and the next thing he knew he was waltzing about the dance hall holding the most beautiful girl in the room in his arms.

It seemed that she was a typical new girl in town, finding her feet. It had been a smart move for her to hook up with the sheriff, and after that night she kept the relationship between them warm but jokey. Flint, who was ultimately a serious man but one who could see the funny side of things, could not make her out at all. She seemed to enjoy his company, flirted with him all the time, had kissed him long and hard – but had never gone any further.

She seemed to fill his thoughts more and more. He was seeing her that very night for a meal in her home. He didn't know yet whether she was his girl or not, but it was certainly begining to look that way and on the whole he was happy with the situation.

He was strolling by the mission as he thought all this. The mission was run by the Sisters of St Xavier. The buildings, grouped together in a seemingly haphazard way, consisted of a chapel with adobe and brick walls, a long hall, living quarters, and a small hospital run by the sisters. They were funded by means of a variety of collections and charitable giving, along with larger gifts from patrons. The sisters were not full nuns, but wore a simple white robe and a large hood with a dark line running around it; they could put this over their heads when it was cold or when they were out in public.

One of the sisters was outside the mission at this very moment, feeding corn to some of the speckled hens that were scratching about in a fenced-off area beside the church hall. Her figure was rather dumpy and he immediately recognized Sister Theresa, who was a force to be reckoned with in the community. She spotted him walking along and immediately waved to him, then lifted the hem of her robe so that she could climb over the fence, revealing her wooden sandals in the process. She smiled at him.

'Why, Sheriff Flint, good to see you again.' She

squinted up at him against the sunlight.

'Good to see you, Sister Theresa. Keeping busy, I see.'

'The Lord's work is never done; even the chickens are part of his great plan for us all. Have you asked that young lady of yours a certain question or not?' She could be very blunt.

'She's not really my "young lady" as you put it, ma'am. We're just good friends.'

'I don't think she sees it that way. Snap her up when you have the chance, that's my advice. Well, these hens won't feed themselves.' She went back to her self-appointed task as Flint walked on, the smile he had been giving her becoming rueful as he pondered on her words.

He did not have much time to ponder. A coach and four came jangling down Main Street. Normally such coaches slowed down when they entered the streets of Greenville but this one did no such a thing. The horses were lathered in sweat and their eyes were rolling, a sure sign that something had scared the bejesus out of them. The town was not particularly busy, with just a few people going about their daily business, but it was busy enough for a runaway coach to become a distinct danger.

At the front of the coach, perched on his seat, was the driver. The problem was that instead of holding the reins tightly, as he should, he had let them slacken and get tangled around his still hands. The man was middle-aged with grey wings of hair on either side of his head and a balding pate. He looked as if he was half-asleep or drugged in some way. There was, however, another explanation for his demeanour, which was to become apparent in a short while.

Flint was not about to let anyone become trampled or suffer grief from a runaway carriage. As it came towards him it was evident that if he remained where he was he would be trampled under those hoofs that were thundering so relentlessly upon the ground. He flung himself to one side, waited for the coach to come level with his body, then jumped on to the step that would take him up to the seat beside the driver. It was a dangerous thing to do. The coach was moving so rapidly that if he missed the step and fell forward there was a distinct chance that he would be crushed under the wheels of the carriage.

It said a lot for him that he did not hesitate in his attempt. There was a wooden rail set in the side of the coach for the very purpose of assisting the driver to mount, and his questing fingers managed to find this. He put his left foot on the step, pushed upwards, then found that he was seated beside the semi-conscious man.

Flint snatched the reins from the driver. Luckily the man still had a tenuous hold of most of them. The carriage was heading towards a sharp bend in the street by then and Flint knew that if the horses did not swerve or turn they were going to get hurt, and so were many pedestrians.

'Whoah! Whoah!' he shouted, almost standing on the seat as he tugged at the leathers, 'Whoah!' For a moment he thought they were going to mount the boardwalk and crash right into a hardware store, then the team slewed over to the left and carried on. He shouted 'whoah' a few more times and kept tugging hard, feeling the leathers biting into his hands. There would be marks there later on from his efforts at getting the horses to stop. Then they slowed and came to a frothing, neighing, panting halt.

Flint looked round at the man beside him. The driver, no longer having anything to anchor him to the seat, lurched sideways and fell with a thud to the dusty, alkaline dirt of the street. Flint assured himself that the horses were not going to take off again, then got down from his seat and ran to where the driver lay. Leaning over the fallen man he noticed for the first time that his left-hand side was soaked in blood; he was wearing a dark-red jacket which was why Flint had not noticed the blood at first. It was obvious that the man had been shot and wounded. The weapon had probably been a handgun of some description, if his expert eye were any judge.

A number of spectators had gathered, among them was little Billy Price. Flint looked up at the boy.

'Billy, don't just stand there, go and get some help. We'll have to get him to the infirmary.'

'Sir.' Billy took off on his mission.

'Here, make yourself more comfortable.' Flint took off his wide-brimmed hat, which had shaded his eyes and neck from the sun, and folded it over as a makeshift pillow to raise the man's head. 'Help'll be here soon. What's your name, friend?'

14

'She's there,' sputtered the man, 'the 'burg ... he shot ... the road ... too late quick ... quip ....' The man's voice faded away and his head fell to one side. Flint felt for the pulse on the man's neck and found nothing. He took his hat from under the man's head and covered his face. The man was completely beyond medical help.

As if this wasn't bad enough, Flint heard the sound of a child crying. He thought at first that it might be an infant in the arms of one of the spectators who had gathered round to see what had happened. But he was faced with mostly shopkeepers, assistants and cowpunchers; there wasn't a young child in sight. Flint straightened up, feeling like a very old man, with a dark foreboding in his soul. He went to the side of the dusty carriage and jerked the door open. There was a child all right, a lusty-looking boy of, perhaps, between twelve and sixteen months. He was twisting around and bawling. Worst of all, he was in the arms of a young woman who had suffered a terrible head wound; her long dark hair was matted with blood as she held the child clasped in her apparently lifeless arms.

CHAPTER TWO

The woman was dressed simply in a long dress that might once have been a pleasant shade of yellow before it had become spattered with her own blood. She did not have a jacket or a bag beside her, or any kind of luggage. Flint took these facts in with an eye that was used to analysing a situation quickly. He often had to act swiftly in his job as sheriff of Greenville and he was used to investigating facts in a logical manner. This told him that she had left in a hurry with the child, who was now bawling lustily as he kept up his struggles.

Flint turned fiercely and looked at the gathering townspeople.

'Nothing to see here,' he said, knowing that the *Greenville Sun* would have the story – drawings and all – the very next day.

He was just assessing what to do next when he heard the faintest of groans. The young woman stirred weakly. She wasn't dead after all; nevertheless it was clear that if she didn't get some kind of attention soon she would surely pass away.

'You, you and you,' said Flint to some of the more able-bodied men who had gathered round to gawp, 'help me lift her out, let's get her to the infirmary.' He went into the carriage and gently disengaged the infant from the woman's arms. It was a harder task than he had expected because she had quite a firm grasp of the child. As her infant was pulled free she gave a gasping moan, then subsided again, her lips moving in a wordless mumble.

Flint arranged to have the corpse of the former driver taken to the undertaker, Lawrie. That individual had a whitewashed stone cellar where he kept the bodies of those whom he was preparing for burial. It was about the coolest place around here and, if the mystery wasn't solved, Lawrie would have the job of burying him for the county anyway.

Old Doc Hollins had finished examining the young woman. She was lying on a flock mattress in the infirmary, the simple iron-frame bed the same as the kind used by the sisters for their own needs. Her wound had been cleaned up and her head had been bandaged to stanch the blood that had flowed from her wounds. The sisters, including Sister Theresa who had cleaned her up, had cut away some of her long auburn hair and the doctor had sewn up the wounds in her scalp with catgut. She was dressed in a white shift and her pale hands seemed to float like lilies on the dark surface of her coverlet.

Flint had not been present while she was being looked after. After seeing that she had been taken to the infirmary he had closed the door of the carriage – with the child still inside – and taken it to the livery, where he had given the proprietor a few silver dollars and instructed him to look after the horses. He had also told the man to leave the coach untouched so that it could be examined more thoroughly later.

Then he had picked up the child, who had continued his full-throated bawling as they drove to the livery. No wonder the infant was distressed after what he had gone through: being jangled along at speed in the arms of a near-dead woman, then thrust into the back of an otherwise empty carriage and taken somewhere completely strange. It would have been more than enough to unsettle an adult, let alone a child who seemed little more than a year old. Yet as Flint lifted the child out, discovering that he was rather heavier than he had expected, the child looked into Flint's face, put out his brawny little arms and gave a loud chuckle, instantly winning over the sheriff who thought himself to be so hardened.

'I don't know your name,' muttered Flint as they left the livery. 'Guess I'll call you Hank. Husky Hank, how does that sound to you, kid?' The child gave a cry of laughter at this and pressed into Flint's shoulder. The sheriff had kept the child from going to the infirmary because he knew the perfect person to look after him. Besides, he had a feeling that a mission was not the kind of place where a child would thrive, and the sisters already had enough on their plate with the injured new arrival.

He knocked on the door of the modest clapboard house that belonged to the schoolma'am. It was part of her reward for coming to teach in a place as wild as this. There had been other teachers over the years, but none like her. She answered the door.

'Joe.' She said his name before taking in that he was holding a lively bundle in his arms. Her home was not far from the livery, so he had just walked there carrying the child. One or two people who knew what had happened had looked at him and remarked on this sight as he strode down the main street, but he was a man on a mission. He had a baby to find a carer for and that baby should be looked after by a woman. *He* had more urgent and better things to do.

'Joe, what's going on here?' asked the schoolmistress. She was dressed in a dark jumper and a black skirt. Her hair was a little straggly, unlike the tidy bun worn when she taught in the school, and was hanging down to her shoulders. He thought he had never seen anything as pretty in his life, but he had to focus on the matter in hand.

'Katie-Jo, I need your help. This here child's arrived in town under some mighty strange circumstances. Could you look after him?'

'Joe, I have my work at the school, I have books to read, lessons to study and give to the children and I have papers to mark and grade. I don't have time to look after a baby.' Her eyes sparkled as she looked at the sheriff. She could see that he was immediately disappointed. 'It's all a bit too much.'

'Guess that's it, then.' He shrugged. The living bundle in his arms turned and gave the schoolma'am a cheeky little grin and waved his pudgy fists. Katie-Jo was a sucker for children of all ages.

'He's lovely,' she said. 'Aren't you sweet, little man?' She leaned in, offering a hand and he wrapped one of his chubby, rather sticky fists around her forefinger. 'The trouble is, I still can't take him in. He needs to be cleaned up, too. What's that dried stuff on him?' She peered at the dark stains on the child's coveralls. Flint did not tell her for the moment that she was looking at dried blood.

'May I come in?' he asked, taking off his hat. 'Just for a moment; he's getting kind of heavy.'

'All right, but I won't change my mind.'

She led him into a little parlour. It had some modest furniture, including a red two-seater couch stuffed with horsehair. By the window was a deal table on which she had spread out her books and papers, pencils, inkpot and pens: the tools of her trade.

He sat on the couch and put the little boy down beside him. The child had bare feet and was dressed in a miniature version of a one-piece worksuit made out of dark-blue denim with shiny brass buttons. He immediately gave a big grin and tried to struggle out of the seat, but Flint held him firmly while he spoke to the pretty woman standing in front of him.

'Listen to me, Katie-Jo. There's been some mighty strange goings-on and I have to get to the bottom of them. This kid – Hank, I've named him, 'cause he's so husky – well, he's a real charmer but he needs looking after in a way I can't manage. You look out for him and I'll make sure his costs are looked after by the office.'

'It's not about money,' said Katie-Jo. 'Is he hungry? I can give him some milk, it's fresh today.' She bustled off before Flint could give an answer and came back with a small cup that had a beaker lip.

'I use such things for the younger ones at school,' she said. She knelt in front of 'Hank' and gently fed him the milk, making sure that he did not spill the cup and wiping away any excess milk with a cloth she had also brought through. Joe told her the story of the coach while she fed the child, taking his time even though he was anxious to get on with his investigation.

'Well, I guess it's about time to go,' he said, scooping up the child when Hank had finished his milk.

'That's so,' confirmed Katie-Jo, looking at him with big serious eyes. Then her expression changed and she shook Hank's tiny hand while he gave a gurgle of contented delight. 'Where are you taking him?'

'To Sister Theresa; she's busy nursing the injured woman, but I guess the other sisters'll have a field day with this one.' He headed towards the door.

'Wait!'

He turned and found her looking at him, serious again, but with a glint in her deep green eyes.

'How long will this investigation take?'

'I guess a couple of days if I get on to it. But how

long is piece of string? I guess it also depends on what I find.'

'All right. I'll do it, but I'll have to take him to school tomorrow. You know, I saw an old cot in the storeroom; I think it must have belonged to one of the teachers ...' her voice trailed off, then: 'Just one thing,' she added, coming forward and relieving him of his cheerful bundle.

'Yes?'

'We're still having that meal tonight.'

Now, as he stood in the sick room looking down at the mysterious young woman, Flint knew that he had done the right thing. Not only was the doctor present, but also Sister Theresa. Flint leaned forward and looked at the woman's features. She did not look, to him, like someone who had been toiling hard since childhood. Those hands of hers were white, long-fingered and delicate, while something about her features spoke to him of one who was more used to giving orders than taking them. She looked fairly young to be a mother, but then girls around here became mothers when quite young, although not usually those who were among the better off. There was no certainty, though, that she was the mother of the child.

'Hey,' said Flint, 'I got your baby; he's being looked after right now. He needs you. I called him "Hank" but I guess you have another name for him. Why don't you wake up and talk to me? Help me and you'll help yourself.'

The woman seemed to hear his voice; she stirred and murmured, making a few feeble sounds. Doc Hollins took Flint by the arm and indicated that they should leave the room.

'Wait a minute,' Flint protested, 'she's trying to say something.'

Again the doctor pulled on his arm. It was in Flint's mind to shake him off so that he could lean in and try to hear what the woman was saying, but Sister Theresa was glaring at him now, too, so he gave in to social pressure and went out of the infirmary. There was a shaded veranda outside that went the length of the building. A recovering patient would be able to sit out here, as the sisters often did, out of the way of the glaring sun.

'What did you think you were doing there, Sheriff?'

'Gathering evidence; it's my job. We need to know who did this – and fast.'

'I don't want you agitating this patient,' said Hollins.

'Just trying to get her to speak to me, to say something about what happened to her.'

'Then you want her to die?' Hollins looked at him so gravely, that despite the seriousnesss of the situation Flint almost wanted to smile.

'What, from a few questions? You saw her, she was responding to me.'

'You really don't understand. That woman might have a fractured skull, not just wounds to the scalp,' said Hollins earnestly. 'Hell, Sheriff! I'm just a small-town sawbones, nothing fancy, but I cleaned her up, stitched her scalp and bandaged her. There's not much else I can do except to let the sisters change her dressings and make sure her wound is kept clean.'

'I still need to ask her some questions.'

'It's early stages, that's what. If you agitate her it could well be enough for her to try and fight to get herself awake. What that woman needs now is peace, and as much sleep as she can get while her scalp and her skull knit together. You go stirring her up it can only be bad for her, especially if she worries over the child. Where is he, by the way?'

'He's with Katie-Jo. So you're saying stirring her up will do her more harm than good?'

'I think so, Sheriff. Surely your investigation can wait a few days?'

'No, it can't, but for the sake of the woman I'll look into this in just a day or two.'

The door was still open; he glanced back into the sick room. The woman was now lying there, almost totally still, so that for a moment he thought the Angel of Death had claimed her; then she muttered a few more times. He might have been an investigating officer, but Flint was, first and foremost, a human being. He nodded to the doctor and Sister Theresa and departed from the infirmary.

He had other fish to fry.

The undertaker was a tall man with a calming voice. He was someone whom the sheriff, in the course of his duties, had unfortunately got to know well, since the death rate in these frontier towns was higher than in the settled North.

'Lawrie, I need a favour,' said Flint. 'I realize you're a busy man, but could I have a few minutes to look at your latest client?'

'Aye,' said the undertaker in his Celtic way, 'come wi' me.'

He took up a lamp that he had lit promptly on the sheriff's arrival and led the way down a short flight of wooden steps to the cellar. This makeshift morgue was the coolest place in town, so sheltered that visitors could feel the temperature drop by several degrees as they stepped down. Flint felt his skin rise in goosebumps and the hairs on the back of his neck prickled. It wasn't the presence of death that bothered him: he had seen plenty of men die in plenty of circumstances; it was just the cold and the stillness of the place that disturbed him. Lawrie set the lamp on a shelf, and while he was doing this Flint took his time to look around the room.

The walls had been whitewashed to give the place a brighter feel, but it only served to heighten the feeling of cold. It was a lot more roomy than he had expected. Two thin stone slabs had been set up on wooden trestles to allow the undertaker to do his work. There was no indication of how he took his clients up and down the steps, but Flint had a sudden vision of them being hauled over his brawny shoulders when they needed to go up for display in their coffins.

One of the stone slabs was unoccupied but on the other, still wearing his pants, though naked from the waist up, was the body of the coach driver.

'I didnae have time to do much wi' him,' said the undertaker with a grim smile. 'He was a hard one to get in here. Was a well-fed man in life, I can tell ye.'

Now that they were close to the man Flint looked at the body. The dead driver was past middle-age and balding, looking peaceful in death in a way that he had probably rarely known in life.

'The question is, did you find anything on him that would give a clue as to who he was or where he came from?'

'He had a couple of silver dollars and some pennies in his pockets, but otherwise not a thing. He could have dropped straight frae the sky.'

'Well, he didn't; he rode into town.'

The lack of anything identifying the man was not that surprising. Flint took a long, hard look at the wound in the man's side. It did not look that bad. He had seen men with far more extensive damage who had lived on to tell the tale: men with missing limbs or gaping wounds from bullets that had torn straight through them.

'So, based on your professional opinion, Lawrie, what do you think killed him? This doesn't look that bad.'

'First of all, Sheriff, it looks to me as if the man was shot at by someone on foot.'

'What makes you think that?'

'I've seen a lot of entry wounds in my time when

26

I've been dressing folks for their funerals. It's no' an uncommon way to go around here. I'd say from the way the powder has burnt his skin and the angle of entry, the bullet or bullets went in and up the way. You'll know as well as I do that it's far better for a bullet to come oot than stay in.'

'What are you trying to say?'

'Once it was in there it would do a lot of damage – a lot; who knows what vital organs it grazed? I'm even surprised he survived until he got intae town.'

'What do you think really happened?'

'I'd say he drove hell for leather away from whatever was happening. A wee bird tells me you've got a young woman set to become one of my patrons if she doesn't recover in the next few days. He was driving away from that situation when someone who did the deed tried to stop him but for some reason the villain didnae ride after the man and finish the job.' He squinted at the corpse in a professional manner. 'I'd say if you opened him up you would see that he had a lot of bleeding on the inside.'

'I see.'

'In effect, he drooned in his own blood.'

'Thanks,' said Flint. 'I think I've learned all I need to know. You've been a real good help, Lawrie.' He turned to leave.

'Wait a meenit,' said the undertaker.

'Yes?' Flint paused, his foot on the first stair.

'What's going to happen about your man here?'

'Ah.' Flint scratched his head. 'I suppose you'll have to bury him. Don't worry, the county'll pick up the tab. I'll make sure of that.'

'They better,' said Lawrie. 'It's not cheap, ye ken, with all the labour involved and that.'

'Thanks again.'

Flint left, having made the man a promise he intended to keep. He was just glad to get outside the undertaker's building.

It was now well past noon and the sun was a blazing ball of light in the sky. A sensible man would have been having a siesta right now to set him up for the rest of the day ahead, preferably after having a cool beer, but Flint had no time for either of those things. Even though his head was throbbing and his muscles aching from stopping the coach and carrying what had turned out to be a surprisingly heavy infant, he had to think. His mind turned to the means by which the dead man and the badly wounded girl had arrived here.

The clue was in the coach, it had to be. With a step that was more leaden than light he headed for the livery.

Naturally the hotel that looked the meanest and shabbiest in Greenville was called 'El Gran Hotel'. It was a building that echoed the architecture of the Spanish who had once ruled this territory, with adobe-and-brick walls, outjutting windows and surfaces that had once been painted in bright shades of red and yellow, though now the colours had almost faded away. The wooden sign over the doorway was practically falling off and the words were barely legible. But it was somewhere to stay, and if you were wanting to remain anonymous and needed cheap accomodation The Grand – its English name – was guaranteed to give you both.

A man rode up to the building. He was mounted on the back of a sturdy-looking mustang which was covered in alkaline dust from the trail. The stranger was tall and young; a few women had judged him good-looking in his time. Not that he had much time for seeing women in his line of work. He was wearing a poncho and smoking a thin cigar, which he discarded and crushed under one of his workaday leather boots.

'Say, Juke, we'll get ya sorted out once I see about this,' said the stranger to the mustang. He went through the entrance, the assured manner in which he strode inside suggesting that he had been there in the past. The desk clerk was a Mexican youth called Ramon.

'Ah Señor Ty,' he said, 'you are back.'

'Yeah,' said Ty. 'Guess a man needs a little recreation when he's been on the trail. Suppose I'll book in, stable Juke, then hit the saloons and get a cold Pabst or three in me, then gab with the boys I know in there about the trail.'

'As you say, *señor*, and perhaps see some pretty *señoritas* too?'

'No, I aim to stay away from the gals this time.'

Ty signed in for three days. Three days of rest and recreation before hitting the trail again. It wasn't much, but his life under the stars was enough for him.

29

'A pretty *señorita*, she arrive in town under tragic way. In painted green coach,' vouchsafed Ramon.

'What about her?' asked the cowboy.

'Oh, she looked after by the Sisters of St Xavier. I saw her, she was hurt real bad, blood and all.'

'What colour was her hair?'

'*¿Qué?*'

'I'm asking what colour was her hair?'

'Like strawberry, what I see. But strangest of all – she has baby with her. Baby boy.'

'I see.' Suddenly the cowboy seemed to tire of the conversation. 'Here's my down payment for the room. First floor? Speak to you later, Ramon.' He took his kit, what little of it there was, and dumped it in his room; then he went back outside to see to Juke. There was a look on his features that some would have described as pensive and others as grim, but then he had been riding the trail for a long time. He took his horse towards the livery, a man deep in thought.

CHAPTER THREE

Flint looked the coach over. It was well-made and the rich green paintwork, although a little faded, had been applied by a craftsman. This was no commercial vehicle; it had been constructed for a private owner. He thought long and hard about what he had seen. In his youth Flint had been a voracious reader, moving from little tales of the prairie, to which he could relate, to the more demanding works of William Shakespeare. He owed his progress to a certain lady of his acquaintance, who owned a ranch where he worked, had noted his appetite for the written word and tried to broaden his education.

'All the world is there,' she had told him, alluding to the works of the Bard of Avon. Well, he had struggled his way through *The Collected Works of Shakespeare*, and had taken to heart a few choice phrases and concepts that he could apply to his own life.

'Dusty,' he said to the livery keeper, 'I've looked over this coach and there's not a clue about the owner to be seen. I thought I might find something such as a scrap of paper, but there's nothing in the lining of the seats, where you would often find that kind of thing. Who do you think it belongs to?'

'Don't rightly know,' said Dusty, squinting at said vehicle. 'See, I haven't been here that long; the feller who was here before me – he was a wonder. He'd probably have known if this here coach had been in town before.'

'Really? How can I get hold of him?'

'You can't, 'least not unless you've got a talent for table-tappin'. He's right over there in the local grave-yard. Came out of the Bonny Belle saloon one night, rolling drunk – you know, the place that's got the high steps for the flooding that comes with the rains – tripped over the balcony and broke his neck. They say a drunk never hurts hisself, I guess that little event gave the lie to that one.'

'Well,' said Flint, 'that Shakespeare fellow, he said something in *The Merchant of Venice* that I've never forgot. It was to do with arrows. He pointed out that if you fired an arrow and lost it, the best way was to fire another arrow in the same direction, see where it went and by following the second arrow you would more often than not find the first.'

'Say, this Shakespeare feller was smart,' said Dusty. 'So what does that mean for you, mister?'

'It means, Dusty, that the coach is my arrow.'

Flint knew that before carrying his plan into prac-tice he had to check up on a few things. The first step on his journey involved a certain young lady: he had to go and see Katie-Jo, find out how she was managing with the infant, and tell her the bad news. He knew her infant charge was not something the schoolboard would be pleased with but, as far as he could see, this case would be solved once he'd traced the owner of the coach, so her looking after the child would only be for another day at the most.

He had taken his meal with Katie-Jo and her infant guest the previous evening. Hank had turned out to be the ideal dinner guest, except for now and then playfully throwing one or two of his utensils across the room. Instead of admonishing him and slapping him, as many might have done, Katie-Jo returned the spoon or fork and spoke to him quietly about how he should behave. Strangely enough, he seemed to listen to her raptly, head on one side, before chuckling and doing something else that involved using his sturdy little body.

When Flint took her in his arms afterwards, in the hall, she kissed him briefly.

'Now you get going. I won't get him settled down until you're away,' she said.

'How so?'

'Because he likes you, that's why. He'll stay awake until he falls over if you stay.'

Now Flint was heading for the school building. The children, the offspring of all sorts of people, from shopkeepers to cowboys, were out playing in the dusty streets of the town because it was the midday break. Not all of them attended school all the time, and it was common practice for the sons of farmers not to turn up at all during cropping time, when all hands were needed to bring in the harvest.

He soon found the schoolma'am. She was sitting at her desk at the front of the classroom, marking some papers. Hank was penned up in a cot close at hand, at his feet an empty bottle that had once evidently held milk. Flint went over to the schoolma'am and gave her a peck on the check; she responded by glaring at him.

'Hiya kiddo,' said Flint, picking up the child who had already stretched out his arms to be lifted. 'Whoa! You're heavy. Has she been feeding you bricks?'

'He was up three times last night,' said Katie-Jo. 'Because he was sleeping in a strange place, I expect. I've been tired all morning.'

The sheriff walked in front of her desk, still holding the child, who was beaming all over his plump little face. He really had taken a shine to his rescuer.

'Katie-Jo, I'm going to be blunt; I'm leaving town.'

'What? Why?'

'I guess this little feller and that woman over at the infirmary are two of the reasons – those along with the dead man currently lying down at Lawrie's.'

'But why do you need to leave town?'

'Too many unanswered questions, that's what. 'Sides, if I don't look into this right now we'll never have a chance to get this little guy back home.'

34

'Why would *you* do that? Send someone else.'

'There's no one else to send. I haven't been the sheriff that long, remember. I was elected just a short while before we met at the dance.' He looked around. 'We met in this very room if I remember rightly.'

'You know, when I saw you I thought you were the kind of man I'd like to know. You had a look of . . . strength about you. I can't put it into words. You just seemed to know what you were up to.'

'I've seen a lot in my life; lost a lot of people, too.'

'Well, appoint some deputies, send one of them.'

Hank gave a wicked chuckle, leaned forward and tried to pull her long, fair hair.

'No, bad boy,' she protested.

'Is that me you're talking to or the kid?'

'Both, if you want to look at it that way.'

'Say, I can't understand why you're getting so worked up about this; a man has to do his job.'

'You're right, you have to do your job. Don't let some little schoolteacher stop you in your tracks.'

'Hey, Katie-Jo, it won't be long, then this'll be behind us and we can just get on with our lives. I have to carry out a task, that's all.'

'Like you said, there's a badly injured woman, a dead man and a homeless child. Nothing to worry about, really.'

He was about to react to her tone, which had sounded a trifle bitter, then he bit back his words. She got up, took the child, slid the hefty infant into his high-sided cot and picked up a brass bell from her high desk. She started ringing with a vigour that suggested she wished she was wringing the sheriff's neck. Evidently the discussion was at an end. He went forward to kiss her one last time and her lips found his with an unexpected passion; then she pulled back as the first of the children began to come through the wide doors.

'Look after yourself,' she said.

'You too.'

Her answering smile was weak.

He bent down and chucked Hank under the chin.

'Watch out for her, kiddo,' he murmured, at which the child gave a delighted chuckle, holding out his sturdy little arms. Flint straightened up, and nodded to the schoolteacher as children streamed in and started sitting at their desks.

Then he walked out without looking back.

When he got to the infirmary he was met by a glare from Sister Sister Theresa. She might have been shorter than he was by about a foot and a half, but she was a formidable woman when it came to protecting those around her from what she saw as a harmful intrusion.

'What do you want, Joe Flint?' she asked.

'I just want to see the injured woman before I go.'

'I won't let you if you are going to start asking her all sorts of questions; she's in no fit state—'

'It's not like that at all.' He took off his hat and held it against his chest, looking much younger as the breeze ruffled his over-long hair. 'I just want to

36

look at her – study her if you like; might pick up something that way – and I don't mean germs.'

'All right, but I'm coming into the sick room with you, and if you misbehave – you're out.'

Sister Theresa opened the door and let him into the infirmary, which was empty, then into the side room where the woman lay. Light entered the room through a simple casement window, which could be opened to let in some fresh air. As Sister Theresa stood near by, keeping a watchful eye on him like a mother hen, Flint went over to the bed.

'She has good times and bad,' said the sister in a low voice. 'There are times when we almost have to prevent her from getting out of the bed even though she's so weak we just need to press her shoulders to keep her from moving. Then there are other times like this when she seems to close to meeting the Almighty.'

Flint said nothing to this, but looked down at the woman. Now that she was properly cleaned up, with her bandages rewound to show more of her face, he could see that she was very pretty indeed.

'We've managed to get some food into her,' said the sister, 'thin beef soup, and milk. We do it through a beaker with a spout and pour the liquid slowly down her throat. We change her too. So she's in no immediate danger of starvation.'

Flint looked again at the young woman, who must, he thought, be less than twenty years old – possibly just over eighteen. Once more he had the impression that she was well-bred and that she had never – until perhaps lately – done a day's work in her life.

Her hands appeared to show some signs of damage – not just on the surface – that seemed to have been sustained over the last few weeks and months; her nails had been cut short, presumably as a matter of practical necessity unless the sisters had done this. It looked to him as if she had been going through a patch in her life that had nothing to do with her upbringing, and he guessed that 'Hank' had a lot to do with this.

The woman muttered a few words, but in such a low voice that he could not hear what she was saying. He leaned over her; even one word might be good enough to give a clue, but there came nothing further.

'Don't worry,' he said, 'your baby is safe. I'm going to help you both.'

Lines of pain and worry had appeared on her forehead. These smoothed out as if she had listened to his words. Sister Theresa started forward.

'That's enough,' she said, and she escorted him out of the room. Once they were outside they stood and faced each other.

'Take care of her,' said Flint. 'I'm going away for a while; I'll catch up when I come back.'

'You do that.'

Sister Theresa did not ask where he was going and he knew immediately that she sensed he was working on the events of the previous day. She put out a hand that was as rough as his own.

'Come back soon.'

'Don't worry, I plan to.'

He put his hat back on, tipped the brim to her, then walked away under the heat of the sun.

CHAPTER FOUR

The horses were harnessed to the carriage. They had been rested and fed for the last couple of days so they were fresh and ready for the journey. Dusty shook his head when Flint appeared.

'You sure about this, Sheriff? Looks to me like you're taking a risk.'

'I don't see what else I can do,' said Flint, 'we've got a genuine 24-carat problem on our hands. If this involves rich people – and from where I'm looking at it does – then sooner rather than later someone's going to come looking for us. It's better the other way round.'

He got up into the driving seat of the coach. He was by no means an expert coachman, but he had been around horses for most of his life and he knew how to handle them. Besides, without any passengers the vehicle was light enough and that meant he would get quickly to where he was going. His own horse, Traveller, was keeping pace beside the coach. Traveller, an appropriate name in this case, was good at acting on his own and he would keep up with the other four because he was unburdened by a rider. It was an unusual arrangement, but Flint had seen it done many times before.

From where he sat he could look right along the road and see the schoolhouse. It was late enough for the children to have gone home, but there was no sign of Katie-Jo. Flint had an uncomfortable feeling that she wanted nothing to do with him at this particular moment. Dismissing the thought from his mind, he looked ahead and cracked the reins. The horses moved at a steady pace and he waved his hat to Dusty and some other townspeople who had noticed he was leaving.

As the carriage turned and headed along the dusty trail that led out of town, a figure with a child in her arms emerged from the school and stood, just watching the departure of a man who had come to mean so much to her in such a short time.

Just a short while later that same day a tall young stranger came into the livery. Dusty recognized him from the day before: a man who had introduced himself only as Ty. The stranger had paid promptly for his mustang to be housed, and Dusty was surprised to see him again after such a short time. Usually when cowboys had time off they spent it with their buddies in the saloons or, during the day, holding horse races across the flat plains outside town.

'Say, old-timer, you got time to talk?' Ty asked.

'I guess,' said Dusty, rolling a cigarette and lighting up. Shooting the breeze with passers-by was one of his favourite occupations.

'Heard a story,' said the stranger. 'Just wondered if it was true.'

' 'Bout the injured woman?' asked Dusty; then, immediately answering his own question, 'Sure, that's true if it's what you're talking about. Happened just the day before you arrived. Hell! You might have noticed the coach sittin' around.'

'I guess I didn't.'

'Right enough. Sheriff Flint got it left at the back of the building, away from prying eyes. Well, it's gone now.'

'Guess you could fill me in on a few details,' suggested Ty.

Dusty told him the story of the coach arriving and how Sheriff Flint had prevented a major amount of carnage in the centre of town, and about the discovery of the young woman and the infant.

'So,' the cowboy drew on a thin black cigar, expelling a trickle of smoke between lips that had gone thin, 'tell me about the woman. Where is she right now? With the Sisters of St Xavier?'

'Mister, you've answered your own question.'

'So what kind of state is she in? It all sounded pretty bad. Is she talking?'

'Don't rightly know about that,' said Dusty. 'As far as I can gather she's not doing that well, but I don't have all that much contact with what's happening there. Guess if she had started speaking the sheriff

42

would've told me.'

'What do you mean: *the sheriff would've told you?*'

'He's been keeping on top of the whole thing. You got to admire that man, he's a real go-getter, makes everyone feel safer when he's around.'

'That's good,' said the young man, 'real good, but you're pretty sure she ain't spoke a word yet?'

'Nope, but Sister Theresa would know. So what are you all about, mister? Why the interest in something that's got nothing to do with you?'

'Guess I was just bored,' said Ty. He flipped a silver dollar at the livery keeper. 'Thanks for the chat, old-timer.' He flicked the remains of his cigar to the ground and was soon gone.

Sister Theresa was carrying out one of her multifarious duties. The mission was not just a place of worship, it was a community with some twenty sisters in all, most of whom rarely went beyond the precincts of their little world except to give people assistance in their dying moments, or to speak to patrons. It was a life of austerity, where the only things guaranteed were three square meals a day, getting up at first light in the summer or at five in the winter to pray, and the endless task of helping others while preserving their own buildings. These sisters, in their black-and-white robes, were mostly women who were not in the first springtime of their years, but that did not mean that they were not able to defend what was theirs, or do what was right.

A tall, young cowboy approached the mission. He

was wearing a gun at his side, but then most cowboys did. His clothes were fairly new: dark trousers and red waistcoat over a white shirt, and he looked fairly respectable; only his calloused hands and the deep tan on his face showed that life had already dealt him a good deal of hard work, and possibly trouble.

Sister Theresa stepped out as he knocked on the old pine door of the mission.

'Have you come to pray? The chapel's round the corner.'

'No, ma'am.'

'I'm no one's ma'am! Call me Sister, or Sister Theresa.'

'I'll visit chapel another time perhaps, Sister.' The young man took off his hat and held it against his chest.

She could see that he was tall and good-looking, the kind of quiet-talking cowpoke who could set a girl's heart a-flutter.

'I'll cut right to the chase, ma'am – I mean Sister. I hear you have a patient in your sick room. She came here in real unusual circumstances.'

'Do you know who she is? Are you a relative?'

'If she's who I think she is, then I think she's been in danger. I just need to see her, talk to her, find out if she's the same person.'

'And who do you think she is?'

'I don't rightly know, that's the thing; not every-thing's clear to me. If I could just talk to her. . . .'

'The young lady is in a poor state of health, she can't talk to anyone. Least of all some cowboy who just expects to stroll in and gawk at a poor woman who's hovering between this world and the next.' It was obvious that they had reached some kind of impasse, and that the young man, who did not seem to be the fastest thinker in the world was trying to get past this gatekeeper to the prize beyond.

At this moment Katie-Jo appeared, bearing Hank in her arms. It was obvious that she wanted to discuss matters with Sister Theresa and, casting only a brief glance at the cowboy – for he was young and good-looking – she stepped forward to address the sister.

'Sister, I want to talk to you about the baby. I think it's time he saw his mother, and that she heard him.'

Hank seemed to know he was under discussion and he gave a wild chuckle and waved his arms. He was wearing an overall made of blue denim and a red shirt. His hands looked as if they were a little sticky from his last meal.

'That's fine, my dear; you can come inside, this gentleman is just leaving.'

'So where is this infirmary, round 'bout the side?' said the stranger, with a sudden look of anger. ' 'Taint right you deny me a reasonable request.' He made as though to go round the side, but Katie-Jo, despite carrying her lively burden, was ahead of him; she marched round the corner too and placed herself firmly in front of the black-painted side door that led to the small infirmary. Hank gave a delighted chuckle at this sudden halt in their progress; he blew bubbles of spittle between his lips and burbled as he gazed at the angry cowboy. Sister Theresa, panting a little as befitted her build, arrived and took up her stance beside the schoolteacher.

'Where do you think you're going?' demanded Katie-Jo of the young man.

'You ladies oughtta let me in,' said the cowboy. 'I just want to see her, that's all.'

'She's not seeing anyone,' said Sister Theresa. The commotion had brought forth some other members of the mission: five in all. Some of them were younger and of a far more impressive build than their leader. One particularly large lady carried a broomstick, the brush normally used for sweeping flagstones, but she looked as if she was quite capable of using the stick end between his shoulder blades.

'Now, Sister Juarez, no violence,' said Sister Theresa. The women lined up against the stranger, showing no fear at all. For a moment his hand dropped towards his gun, a tried-and-true instinctive way of dealing with an enemy, then he grabbed his hat and jammed it on his head.

'This ain't over. I'll see her, you'll see if I don't.'

'Don't come back,' said Katie-Jo, speaking for them all, at which Hank made a buzzing noise between his lips that sounded faintly mocking. Everyone laughed. The young man's back stiffened but he did not turn and soon he was gone from sight.

CHAPTER FIVE

Meanwhile, Flint had made good time getting to Afton. It wasn't a huge distance, as distances go, but it wasn't the best road in the district and he had to watch out for ruts in the road in case a wheel went down too far and broke apart, or a horse turned a hoof and damaged a leg. Given these hazards it seemed nothing less than a miracle that the original driver had not fallen off on his desperate flight away from danger.

On the edge of town stood a big house built in the colonial style so favoured by the rich. It had three floors, sash windows with green-painted shutters that could be pulled over against the elements, a wide, raised porch at the front with a seat varnished a deep brown colour, its back padded with brown cushioning; here the owner could sit in the evening with a view of the road. The mansion was surrounded by solid adobe walls, with some fencing atop, and a broad drive at the side. There was stabling for horses and carriages.

Flint had his suspicions about the building, which he reckoned belonged to Douglas Quinn, the respected businessman about whom he had heard so much, but the place looked and felt somehow empty even on the cursory examination he made in passing.

Soon he was in the town itself. Afton had a more settled air than Greenville. The main street contained a wide range of shops, including hardware stores, general stores and cafés. The population of the town, although modest, was at least double that of the place he had just left. Of course Afton had the railway, which made a major difference to any town. Ironically, in a period of just three short years, the town had boomed because the railways had attracted a huge increase in the arrival of animals in the cattle-export business and the amount of goods that could be brought here or taken away in a two-way traffic.

Many of the buildings he was now looking at, the red-stone ones, would not have looked out of place in New York, and these too were products of the coming of the railways, along with the ability to support a booming population. Flint should have felt like the country cousin, but this was not his attitude at all. He was here for a purpose.

He halted the coach and four in the main street and went to see the sheriff, Ben Couhard. Couhard's office on Silver Street, off the main drag and named after one of the local industries, was in a two-storey building that made Flint's single block office seem like a poor relation. A town with a bigger population had bigger law-and-order problems, so it was only to be expected that the taxpayers would put more funds into the business of keeping the town free of miscreants.

Ben Couhard was sitting behind his desk when Flint knocked at the door and walked into the office. He was a big, solid man in his early fifties who wore black trousers, a dark-blue shirt and an equally dark cloth waistcoat, with his badge of office taking pride of place on the left breast pocket.

'Good day, Ben,' said Flint heartily.

'Good afternoon to you, sir,' said Ben, struggling out from behind his desk. Again Flint felt a pang of envy. This man had several deputies who did most of the work.

'So, jest a social call is it, son?' asked Couhard, beaming and pumping his visitor's hand.

'No, I'm in town on business,' said Flint. 'Got something to show you, if you care to take a look outside.'

'Sure; hasn't been busy here for a while,' said Couhard. On the way to the coach Flint explained the circumstances in which it had arrived in Greenville. The Afton sheriff, who had been smiling as they went out, gradually lost his cheerful attitude and became somewhat brisk and professional. What was more, an expression of concern came over his face when he saw the coach.

'You know who it belongs to?' pressed Flint, seeing the expression of alarm now written large on the man's face.

'It's – it's Quinn's,' said Couhard. 'Just wait right

there. I have to go and get someone.' He scuttled off down the street and came back with a tall man who was dressed in a black suit and wearing a tasteful grey-silk tie. The new arrival was at least the same height as Flint, who was not small, and he looked very cool and relaxed. He had a shock of dark hair with some grey at the sides. He looked to be in his early forties, and he had the appearance of a professional man: the type who wore white shirts and cologne, had clean fingernails and very white teeth. Flint disliked him on sight.

'There you go, Mr Parker,' said old Ben, a little too respectfully for Flint's liking. 'I thought it would be the one. I remember Mr Quinn—'

'That's fine, Ben,' Parker stopped him short; there was an edge to his voice that Flint did not like. Flint did not show this on the surface and was careful to keep his expression neutral.

'I'm Sheriff Joe Flint of Greenville,' he said by way of introduction. 'Do you know who this carriage belongs to?'

'I do,' said the stranger. 'My name is Nat Parker, agent for Mr Douglas Quinn, leading citizen of this town, and this carriage belongs to my employer.'

'Well, that's mighty interesting,' said Flint. 'Perhaps you can explain to me how this rig ended up in my town with a dead man on board.'

'A dead man?'

'The driver.'

'Was there anybody else on board?'

'As a matter of fact there was, a young woman,

nearly dead herself, and an infant.'

Was it his imagination or was Flint right to suppose that the immediate but fleeting expression on Parker's face suggested that the agent was not surprised by this last piece of information? Flint might not have been rich, or particularly well-placed, but he knew people, and he was certain that he had seen something that was gone almost as soon as it had appeared. Then Parker's too-handsome face took on that smug expression again.

'Well, that's no concern of mine; I'm just glad to have my employer's coach back.'

'How do I know you're telling the truth, Mr Parker?' Flint was not just talking about the coach and they both knew it, though Nat Parker pretended otherwise.

'I can assure you, Mr Flint—'

'That's Sheriff Flint to you, Mr Parker.'

Well I can assure you, *Sheriff*, that this carriage belongs to my employer. He was going to use it but found that it had been stolen. What happened from then owards is none of my business until the return of the property.'

'So a dead man, a dying young woman and a potentially orphaned infant have nothing to do with you at all?'

'Sheriff Flint, you surely don't need to continue with this line of questioning,' said Couhard, putting his not inconsiderable bulk between the two men so that they both had to step back to avoid having their toes stepped on. 'Mr Parker is a leading citizen of this town. He's not used to being questioned like this.'

'When a crime has been committed that affects the lives of people to this extent, I think I'm entitled to ask a few questions, Ben. Isn't that so, Mr Parker?'

'I'll get one of my men to take the coach back to my employer's home,' said Parker, 'and I thank you on his behalf, Sheriff Flint. You have done a good job of work here.' He stepped aside, nodded to the two men and began to walk away. Flint was used to this kind of trick from those who just wanted to get away from a situation. He wasn't about to let the smooth Nat Parker walk away from this one.

'It ain't finished, Mr Parker; I want to speak to your employer personally.'

'What?' Parker turned and stared at Flint as if astonished that he was still there.

'A coach and four that was stolen? It seems to me that someone can steal a gewgaw from a man's house and it might take him a month of Sundays to notice it's gone,' said Flint, 'but if something like this is stolen there's bound to be a ruckus like no other.'

'Look,' Parker spread out his hands, 'Mr Quinn, he's had other things on his mind; he asked me to report the matter to Sheriff Couhard here – didn't he, Ben?'

'That's right,' said the older sheriff. 'But we had a bad situation here; the Clancy brothers was robbing a bank at the time and we was all engaged in fighting them – a real shoot-out, but we got them in the end. That was just about the same time the coach was took.'

'See what I mean?' said Parker smoothly. 'The sheriff and his men had a lot on their plate.'

Parker noticed that Flint was staring at him with an expression like that of a mule that isn't about to shift, despite its owner's pleas for to get it moving.

'All right,' Parker conceded, 'come and visit Mr Quinn tomorrow. This is something I need to set up, and it's late afternoon now. His health isn't too good and he goes to bed early. His mansion is just at the edge of town.'

'I know where it is,' said Flint.

'Good. I'll see you there at ten in the morning, then you can be on your way.'

Parker departed to return to his day-to-day concerns.

'At least it's out of your hands now,' said Ben, nodding his head towards the coach. 'His men will take it away and that'll be the end of the matter.' He looked at Flint's grim expression and suddenly gave a loud laugh.

'What's so funny?' demanded Flint.

'You. You're like a bulldog chasing a juicy steak. Come back to my office and I'll get you a java.'

'I guess I could do with something; it wasn't an easy trip.' Flint stubbornly waited where he was until Parker reappeared from further along the street with two ranch hands, barely in their twenties, who looked as if they thought they were hard enough to take on all comers. With barely a glance at Flint, Parker got them to take the conveyance away.

'See you tomorrow, Sheriff,' he said as the wheels

rattled across the ground. 'Don't forget.' He again took his departure. The lawmen walked away in the other direction.

As they drank their coffee Ben looked over his steaming mug at Flint.

'What got into you there? Questioning Nat Parker like that?'

'Don't rightly know.' Flint took out his gun and examined the barrel. 'Clean as a whistle,' he said thoughtfully.

'Hell! What you doing that for? Nobody's gettin' shot,' said Ben, a little nervously.

'Somebody did,' answered Flint, 'and someone brutally attacked a young woman. Care to hazard a guess as to who she might be? For instance, did Quinn have a daughter?'

'He didn't just have a daughter; matter of fact he had a son too.'

This was more like what Flint wanted to hear. Couhard seemed to be thinking about what he wanted to say next. His words, when they came, were not a total surprise to Flint, who had guessed that, although he seemed to be a welcome guest in the sheriff's fancy office, in truth he was just there so that Couhard could keep an eye on him.

'Joe, I'm asking you as a fellow lawman: don't get too involved with Nat Parker. He's a powerful man around these parts. He won't let you go about stirring things up just when he's got them the way he wanted.'

'That so?' Flint set down his cup and stood up.

'Thanks for your hospitality, Ben. Mighty fine cup of coffee, but I guess I'd better get out on the town, do a little footwork and make sure that my horse is rightly fed and watered.'

You're welcome to stay for the night,' said Ben. 'Plenty of room, and the wife won't object to the company.'

'Kind of you to offer, Ben, but I guess this ain't a social visit.'

True to his word, he made sure that Traveller was seen to at the livery, then went on into town. He had noticed before that though the main streets of Afton seemed a lot more respectable than those of Greenville the back streets were just as untidy, with adobe-and-wood buildings constructed seemingly at random across the rough landscape towards the mines. Flint guessed he could walk these streets and ask a few questions if he wanted, but his instinct was to head towards the town's main saloon, the Silver Dollar, a name that acknowledged the metal that had led to the town's prosperity.

Afton was a place where people who had been building did not want their property to abut hard against their neighbours; space was not at a premium. Flint was passing a shadowy alleyway when he heard a quiet voice.

'Hey you, Sheriff Flint!' He looked to one side; there was a man in the shadows, his face could not be made out. 'I got some information for youz, about Nat Parker.'

'Really?' Flint stepped towards the man, into the

darkness of the alleyway. That was a big mistake because he felt a crashing blow on the back of his head. He tumbled towards the ground with a sickening realization that his journey to Afton might have ended for good.

CHAPTER SIX

He came to with a start. When he tried to get up he discovered that far from lying on his back he was sitting on one of the bentwood chairs in the sheriff's office. The back of his head was aching, and when he felt around with his hand he found that his scalp was still faintly sticky from where it had been bleeding. As his eyes started to focus he found that he was looking at the somewhat overweight frame of Couhard, who was staring back at him as a man visiting an art gallery might look at an exhibit of which he is not too enamoured.

'So, we meet again,' said Flint, avoiding asking the obvious question.

'Luckily I was uptown on other duties,' said Couhard. 'I saw what was happening. There was two of them; they was intent on robbing you – didn't even give you a chance of getting your gun.'

'Robbing me? Sure, that was the reason, except the one who spoke to me knew my name.'

'So what?' Couhard spread out his hands. 'You

might be a stranger in town but you were mighty vocal when you were uptown; anyone could have heard us discussing things near Quinn's coach. You had left it just outside a hardware store if I remember. Wouldn't be difficult for someone in bad form to pick up on you.'

'Did you get them?'

'Well, gee, that's the problem. When I shouted and came over they scuttled off like the rats they were. I figured you could be hurt real bad so I fired a coupla warning shots after them and they vanished into the back streets. I examined you, found out you weren't at death's door and brought you back here again with the help of a good citizen. How do you feel?'

'I'll tell you in a minute.' Flint rose from his seat and felt as if someone had crashed a giant hammer on top of his head. He suppressed an exclamation of pain, winced and sat down again. 'Guess I'll just take it easy for a couple of minutes before I'm on my way,' he said.

'On your way? I guess you mistake what's happened to you. I've seen cases like this before: man gets a blow to the head, pretends it's all fine and walks out the door, next thing he's passed right out again in the middle of the road. No siree, you're getting a hot meal in you, and staying upstairs tonight.'

Flint was in a mood to argue with the sheriff but he had to admit that the thought of some hot food and a warm bed was tempting. Back in Greenville the small boy was in safe hands, the young woman was getting the best care she could have, and the dead man was going to stay dead. He gave the sheriff a weak smile.

'I guess I'll take you up on that offer, Ben; no harm done.'

'I'll tell the wife.'

That very night, back in Greenville, a man sat thinking about the choices he had to make. There was a woman who might or might not wake up and tell everything she knew to the authorities. He was not an overly imaginative man, but he knew that if the circumstances of what had happened to her came to light he would be punished by the man who had hired him; at the very worst he would pay for his mistake with his life.

The bed was not exactly the most comfortable that he had ever reclined upon but it was not his choice of bed that was causing him to lose sleep. He had been hired to finish a job and that was what he was going to do. Not tonight: he was still sore from riding the trail and hiding from the very authorities he was about to defy. This did not mean that he was unable to make a trip into town and do his homework. The exercise would do him good, and might even allow him to snatch a few extra hours of shut-eye, which he would need if he was to be alert and ready for his task.

The desk clerk was no longer in the hallway. El Gran Hotel was not living up to its name, but at least that meant that he was not observed as he left the building.

Luckily for him it was a weekend, so the town was filled with a lot of cowboys who had come in to spend their hard-earned dollars; consequently the streets were busy. Unlike the cowboys he had no compadres; once more he had been left alone. He gulped a little enviously as he passed the saloon: a drink would have gone down well, but this was another pleasure he would deny himself until his task was complete.

Soon he was at the clustered buildings of the mission. His left leg was sore now and he dragged his foot a little. He was in pain, of that there was no doubt.

'All caused by you, you bitch!' he said between gritted teeth. He already knew which building was the little infirmary, that it held six beds and that there was a side room. He found the window for the side room easily enough and confirmed that, as he had thought, it was a casement window with a catch on the inside.

He could picture her now, lying there on the bed all silent and white. He took out his Bowie knife and tested the edge on his thumb; one second was all it would take once he was inside. One slash across the throat and she would never tell anyone anything again. He slid the blade of the knife through the tiny gap between window and sill. Just as he had thought, it would be easy enough to lever up the catch and a moment later he would be inside to carry out the deed.

But not tonight: the town was too full of roistering cowboys. He had to snatch back his knife and conceal it as a group of them passed close by. Luckily they were too drunk and arguing too much with each other to pay him any attention. But there were others in the district at the moment who were not as drunk, and who might spot him going away after the deed, and that would not do. After all, he was doing this for money, not revenge. But as he turned to leave and a sharp pain shot through his leg he smiled at the thought.

Revenge wouldn't be so bad, either.

CHAPTER SEVEN

When Flint woke up in the morning he felt as if he had the worst hangover of his life. This was no mean comparison since he had experienced more hangovers than he'd had hot dinners at one point in his career. There was a lump the size of a hen's egg on the back of his head, a lump that was tender to the touch. He was not going to be much good for the rest of that day. To his consternation he found that he had to let himself take it easy, spend a short time in Ben's office, then go back to bed.

Before doing this, he had a local kid pass a message to Nat Parker that the visit to Quinn's would have to be postponed until the following day at the same time. It cost him half a dollar.

Another night passed. This time when he awoke he felt much better; most of the sickness had gone and he was almost his normal self. A blow like that to the head was bad. A mite harder, it could have killed him.

Couhard was up good and early as he always was,

and he cast a concerned look at Flint over the strips of bacon and newly baked bread that made up his breakfast: Flint had declined any food, although he loaded up on coffee.

'Guess the best thing you can do is go back to Greenville,' said the older man, 'I'll take care of things at this end. Old man Quinn won't take long to question and I'll get one of my deputies to relay the result to you as soon as possible.'

A lesser man might have capitulated. After all, what did he have to lose? It would be so easy to let the Afton sheriff take over – this was his jurisdiction – and when your head felt as if it was still tender and a crashing headache threatened to come back at any second you might as well take advantage and go for an easy life.

'No thanks,' said Flint. 'Much quicker if I just go over and see him. Matter of fact, it's about time.' He finished his coffee and grabbed some bacon. 'I'll eat this on the way over to get saddled up, if you don't mind.' Then he was out through the door before the other man could protest.

The scrap of food in his belly and the fresh air made a difference as he rode out to the Quinn place. In clear daylight the mansion looked even more forbidding. There was no sign of the coach. Parker was waiting for him outside the building as Flint tied his horse's reins to the hitching post set outside for visitors.

'Well, Sheriff Flint, this is a pleasure,' said Parker. 'I wasn't expecting you to arrive so promptly.'

'Why would that be, Mr Parker?' asked Flint. It was an innocent-sounding question, but they both knew that the answer could infuriate one man and reveal the possible criminal behaviour of the other. Parker, of course, was much too wily to give anything away.

'Come inside. It's not one of his good days, I'm afraid, but he will see you. I will ask that you leave when he wants you to go.'

'Of course,' said Flint. He did not mention that his head was starting to throb once more and that he was feeling sick and weary again, the effects of the fresh air having worn off a little.

The atmosphere inside the building was distinctly musty, which told him that this was not a place that was aired much. He was led into a large room filled with mementoes of a long life, with trophies – mainly heads of deer, antelope and cougar – hanging on the walls, along with different types of hunting weapons. The only pictures were drawings and paintings of open country, some with beeves and cowboys: the landscape of Quinn's youth. The room was noticeably dark.

Douglas Quinn sat on a large armchair that was upholstered in a red plush velvet fabric. He had a shawl on his knees and it was obvious from one glance at his features that this was a man looking older than his years. Beside him stood a youngish woman with her hair in a bun, who wore a long dress and a plain blouse with only a simple pink ribbon bow at the front. It was also obvious that she was his housekeeper.

'Mr Quinn?' asked Flint. The old man lifted his head and looked at the visitor with red-rimmed eyes.

'Yes. What do you want?' Even the man's voice sounded shaky and worn. It was obvious that Quinn was not going to stick around in this world for long.

'My name is Joe Flint, sheriff of Greenville. I just wanted to ask you about your stolen coach. What do you remember about what happened?'

'Nothing, Sheriff. I was ready to go into town and it was taken. That's all.'

'You didn't see anybody or hear anything?'

The old man looked up at his housekeeper-cum-nurse. There was a pleading look on his face.

'Perhaps you should answer the question, Mr Quinn,' said Flint.

'Mr Quinn has problems with his memory,' said the nurse, who was in her early thirties, and was not a bad-looking woman.

'I just need to talk to him, that's all,' said Flint. 'So, Mr Quinn, how are your children?'

'My children? What's that got to do with it?'

'It's just that I thought there might be a possible connection. You see, there was a young woman in the carriage, badly injured, and an infant. So what does your daughter look like?'

'I don't know what you're talking about.' The old man shifted uncomfortably in his seat.

'Flint, I think you should stop this line of questioning,' said Parker, leaning in towards the sheriff. Maybe it was because the man was wearing some kind of a man-scent, or perhaps because Flint disliked being pushed around by some pomaded dandy, but he pressed on with his line of questioning.

'Yes, your son and your daughter; what's happened to them?'

'Mr Flint, they're both dead,' said Quinn. 'My son, he went bad, he was too full of himself. He went to Santa Fe and got involved with a bunch of lowlifes. He was shot dead in a bar-room brawl twenty years ago. My daughter . . .' his voice trailed off and he looked again at the housekeeper.

'His daughter, Marianne, looked after him here, she was his helpmeet for years.'

'And she's very young?'

'Mr Flint, my daughter died of kidney failure at the age of forty-two.' The old man passed a tembling hand across his face. 'I think it's time you went away, Sheriff. I was going to use my carriage and it was taken, I don't know who did it. Go away.'

'Can't you see the man is tired?' asked Parker. 'He's not well, you should leave him for now.'

The old man was indeed hunched in the chair now, his hands over his face. Flint saw that he was going to get nothing else from him so he nodded to the housekeeper.

'Thanks, Miss . . .'

'Parker,' she said, drawing herself up to her full height. Now Flint could see why she seemed so familiar, since there was a distinct family resemblance.

'Jade is my sister,' said Parker. 'Shall we go, Mr Flint?'

They went outside the building and stood there.

Flint looked around.

'You know, this place is pretty well looked after,' he said. 'The grounds are in order, the lawns look good. I expect there'll be some kind of maintenance going on?'

'I expect so; the housekeeper will negotiate with locals for that,' said Parker, implying that such matters were nothing to do with him. He fixed Flint with those glittering eyes. There was no doubting that Parker was a man with a forceful, compelling personality. 'Now that you've found out everything you need to know I expect you'll be wanting to make your way back to Greenville.'

'Not really. I want to have a little talk with your sister.'

'What?'

'Well, if – as you say – she's his right hand now, I expect she'll be able to tell me when and how his coach was stolen. I can see she's got her hands full at the moment, but it's easy enough for me to stick around and ask her later on today – once Quinn is settled.'

'I think you know everything you need to know. The carriage was prepared for going into town and was stolen, it's as simple as that.'

'Who prepared it? Where was Mr Quinn going? Why was there a young woman inside it?'

'I know what you're going to do,' said Parker. 'I can see it in your eyes. You're going to hang around this town asking questions and raising everyone's hackles. Well, let me tell you, Sheriff, this matter isn't in your jurisdiction. You've brought it to our attention in this town, and we'll investigate on our own. Couhard's a perfectly capable man. Now get out of here and leave a sick old man alone.'

Flint knew better than to argue with one of the richest men in town. There was no point in trying to press an authority that he did not have. He had been elected by the good citizens of Greenville, not Afton, and he was a poor country cousin here.

'Well, Mr Parker, I may be just a border rambler to you, but I like to get answers. So maybe I will leave, but I'll be back.' He jammed his wide-brimmed hat on his head against the heat of the day and unhitched Traveller. It was time to leave, but for the time being only.

CHAPTER EIGHT

Once he was back in town Flint wondered if he should check in to Couhard's office. Then it occured to him – and it was just a passing thought – that this might be precisely what he was expected to do. He had enough money on him to last a couple of days. Instead of leaving his horse in the livery in the main street, he hitched Traveller outside the saloon beside a trough full of water – he would stable him in the livery later – and headed instead to a place where he could eat.

He took off the six-pointed silver badge that he had worn so prominently when he was talking to Quinn. With railways, the stockyards and the mining business all going on, the streets of Afton were busy, but most of the citizens did not give him a second glance and that suited him fine. He could have been any one of the thousands of cowboys who passed through here yearly.

He chose an eatery called 'Papa's' which was situated down a side street. The fare was plain but nutritious: bacon, eggs and beans all washed down with a few cups of coffee. He was not in hurry to leave the place, so he hung around in his seat in the corner, unobserved, but watching and listening all the time. The place was filled with cowboys who were gossiping about their time on the trail, the beeves they had handled, and the difficulty of crossing the various rivers on the way, such as the Pecos.

Their talk aroused a strange ache inside him. He had been one of those men once, sleeping under the stars, travelling hundreds of miles along one or other of the trails that marked the progress of cattle to the northern markets and to the Indian reservations. In many ways he would have given his money and position to be one of them again; it was a lot less complicated than whatever this was that he had been landed with.

He stayed for well over an hour until he felt more like his old self. The throbbing at the back of his head had settled down to a mild ache and he could only thank Providence that the blow had not broken his skull. He was sure in his mind about one thing: no one would catch him out in the same way again. He had made the mistake of thinking that Afton, with its fine red-brick buildings instead of the wood-and-adobe of Greenville, was a civilized place, when really, underneath, it was just the same kind of rat-infested burg, where the inhabitants could cut up just as rough.

It was with this thought in mind, and his body feeling as good as he was going to get it for now, that he left the eatery and headed back towards the post to which his horse was tethered.

Without formulating the matter too boldly in his own mind he decided that he was going to house Traveller in the livery, then take a look around to find out what he could about several matters. He was going to investigate Nat Parker, including any holdings that the man might have. He was going to go back to the mansion belonging to Quinn, and this time he was going to question Parker's sister, who had looked as if she had too much of a hold on the old man.

First, though, he was going into the saloon to listen out for local gossip, perhaps having a couple of cold beers in the process. There was nothing wrong with having a beer on the job, it helped cool you down and slowed time, so that you could appreciate your surroundings and blend in with the people there, not to mention that it was good for refreshing your soul.

This thought was still lingering in his mind as, while he was unhitching his horse preparatory to leading him off, he saw three men further along the boardwalk who were deeply engaged in conversation. There was nothing wrong with that; he knew this was a 'happening' town, where deals were often carried out in the street. The men were all younger than he was by a few years; two seemed vaguely familiar and they were looking in his direction, which immediately suggested to him that he was not about to have an easy time.

He decided to leave Traveller where he was for the time being. He had only just started to unhitch the animal and would not have time to untie him fully and jump on his back if trouble started. He affected not to be interested in the men and actually stepped out on to the road to give them a wide berth as he headed towards the saloon.

'Hey, are you Joe Flint?' asked one of them. 'Come over here, I've got some information that might be of some use to you.'

Flint came a little closer, although still holding well back.

'What is it?' he asked.

'It's about Nat Parker,' said the man, still keeping his voice friendly. This did not fool Flint for one minute because he knew a quote from the Bard that said a man could smile and smile and still be a villain, the truth of which he knew only too well.

'Tell me here and now,' he said.

'Naw, a bit too public,' said the man; his friends were standing beside him, smiling too.

Flint could feel a tingling at the nape of his neck. He knew that he was not about to walk away from the three of them. Sometimes it is better to lance a boil than to let the poison within fester and bubble, so he came so close to them that he was practically at arm's length from their youthful forms.

'If you can't tell me something about a public figure here, then you can't tell me anywhere else, I guess,' said Flint. 'Spill the beans.'

The man lost his smile and Flint saw that he was

getting angry.

'A little too uppity for a stranger, wouldn't you say?' The other two nodded in agreement. 'Let's get him, boys.'

Because he had been waiting for something like this to happen – his senses had guided him well this time – and because he was relaxed but alert, Flint was immediately able to respond to the threat. In truth he knew that these three were working for Parker, and that their talk of that person had just been a ploy to grab Flint's attention and bring him close.

With this in mind he swung to one side as the biggest man – the speaker – lunged at him, a move that would have knocked the sheriff flat to the ground had it not been for the fact that Flint avoided it and let the man's own impetus carry him forward. He smote the man on the back too, and, since the attacker was leaning forward as he ran, this sent the assailant sprawling on the dusty road.

The other two men did not waste any time; they came at him as a pair. He could see right away that they were confident and that they were not going to give any quarter.

The previous morning, when the light of dawn was just filtering through the window, the young woman in the infirmary had opened her eyes. She stared up at the ceiling for a while, with a look on her face that was midway between bewilderment and terror. She lay like this for what must have seemed to her like hours but was only ten minutes or so, then with a faltering hand she pulled back the bedsheets.

She was so weak after her attack and being in bed for so long that she had to hold on to the iron-framed bedstead to stand up. She stood like this for a full minute, the blue gown that she had been clothed in enveloping her like a shroud. She looked around the room again, then began to grope her way towards the door almost as though she were blind.

Sister Theresa, who was always up early for her morning devotions, was in the chapel when her sharp hearing detected movements in the adjoining infirmary. Though it was locked against the outside world the entire complex of buildings was connected by a set of adjoining doors. Taking a brass candlestick in hand – for she was not above defending what she saw as the rights of her mission – the Sister of St Xavier quietly opened the door and stepped into the infirmary. She gasped and nearly dropped the candlestick when she found herself apparently confronted by a ghost. Then common sense asserted itself and she knew at once that she was looking at her patient.

The woman opened her mouth but no words came out. Sister Theresa guided her to her simple toilet, then took her back into the room, barely saying a word the whole time except to speak in a low, reassuring voice:

'Don't worry, things have been bad, you've had a hard time, but you're amongst friends now.'

The woman looked around the small room in which only a crucifix and some coloured prints adorned the otherwise bare walls.

'You're safe,' said Sister Theresa.

'No, not . . . Papa,' said the woman. 'Papa,' she repeated, looking around again. Then suddenly weariness seemed to engulf her once more and she sank down upon her bed. Sister Theresa left her then, only disturbing her later, but in a comforting fashion, when she awoke again, and babbled a few incoherent words before dropping off once more. The fact was, Sister Theresa thought, if she could react in this way, even if only with her vague utterances, the girl was already on the mend.

'What's your name?' asked Sister Theresa the second time she went in to see the woman, who looked at her for a few seconds with apparent comprehension. However, she ignored the question and looked around with questing eyes that took in the room as she searched for some kind of unknown danger. Sister Theresa asked again, but still this did not draw a response from the woman.

'Where's baby?' she asked, 'I need my baby.' Then she fell back on the bed again, once more unconscious with the strain of terror and loss. To those who knew little or nothing about medicine it would have seemed that the woman was in a bad way, but Sister Theresa knew better; she could see the signs of vitality flowing back into her young guest. Perhaps it was time for her to be reunited with her baby, even if only for a little while.

The woman's returning vitality was a testament to her youth. In a way Sister Theresa envied her.

Whatever her name was.

Flint knew at once that if he was going to gain an advantage over these two he was going to have to fight low and he was going to have to fight dirty. He sensed that, in the arrogance of their youth, they thought they were going to make short work of this stranger whom they had been told to attack. One of the young men was over six feet tall, so Flint immediately kicked out and cracked him on the knee, following on from this by snaking out his foot and pulling at the man's good leg. The stranger fell backwards on to the boardwalk with a good solid thud. His curses rang in the air.

'You didn't ought to have done that,' said the man's companion with a snarl worthy of a pit-bull. He punched out at Flint and got the sheriff on the side of the head; luckily it was only a glancing blow because Flint, who was keyed up to the slightest movement, had sensed that the punch was coming and jerked his head away.

Flint responded by snatching the gun out of his holster. In a way he would have been perfectly justified in putting a bullet into the man who, after all, was doing his best to inflict damage on a stranger he had never met. However, the gun wasn't loaded; that was simply the way the sheriff worked. He kept his bullets for when he really needed them, and the prospect of a street brawl had not occurred to him when he'd buckled on his gunbelt that morning. Instead of firing he held his Colt by the barrel and gave the only upright attacker a whack on the side of his head, which sent the man reeling as if he had suddenly become drunk.

Flint had forgotten that there was a man sprawled on the dusty road behind him. He was suddenly reminded of this fact when two arms snaked around him from behind and pulled him off the boardwalk upon which he had jumped to deal with his two other attackers.

His back was strong from years of working on the range and riding hard on powerful steeds, so he resisted the efforts of the man to pull him down, knowing instinctively that once he was on the ground he would be finished. The effort to stay upright was all very well, but he was faced with another problem: the man behind him had his forearm so tightly around Flint's neck that the sheriff could feel his air supply being cut off; soon he would weaken and fall to the ground anyway.

Flint had another trick in his armory. Since the man behind him was using his upper-body strength and was employing both arms to try and pull down his opponent, this meant that his legs were unprotected, and the man had long, bony limbs. This was fine with Flint, who had square heels to his boots, made of solid leather. He simply kicked out backwards, put one heel into use and raked it straight down the man's right leg as hard as he could. The shin was a relatively exposed and bony area, with little fat for protection. Flint knew from experience that it would feel to the man as if his leg had suddenly caught fire.

The man gave a gasp of pain and surprise. He was still holding on to Flint but his grip had weakened to the point where Flint was able to shrug off the constraining arms, turn, and punch the would-be conquerer straight in the face. The attacker had not been prepared for things to change so suddenly, and he took the full force of an additional uppercut to his chin. This time when he fell back to the gritty ground it was obvious that this was one cowboy who would not be getting up for a long time.

Flint snatched up his Colt .44, which had fallen to the ground when he was being attacked from behind, and faced up to his two other attackers who were about to rush him again.

'I wouldn't do that, boys,' he said, panting as the heat of the day bore down on him. He was dripping with sweat from his exertions.

Couhard appeared further along the street. He strode along with a speed quite remarkable in an older man who was running to fat. Flint saw him coming towards them out of the corner of his eye and gave a small grunt of satisfaction. It wouldn't be long before these three would be behind bars eating dry bread and counting flies.

Couhard came straight up to the side of Flint and stuck a gun into his ribs.

'Put down the weapon, *mister*,' he said, 'you're under arrest.'

Nat Parker was also in the street. He had appeared

during the fight along with a crowd of excited citizens who had gathered when they saw that a battle was going on. Nat was the first to speak after Couhard made his announcement to Flint.

'What's going on, Sheriff?'

'It looks as if my fellow lawman has bitten off a little more than he can chew.' Couhard told him.

'They started the fight,' said Flint mildly, ignoring the gun sticking into his ribs and turning to look *his* fellow lawman straight in the face. Couhard, confronted by probing eyes, took a step backwards.

'Is that right, boys? Did you attack this here vistor to our fine burg?'

'Nope,' said two of the men almost in unison.

'He just started in on Bud there,' added the younger of the two, 'and we thought we would give Bud a hand.'

'Seems to me your friend got a little uppity in his questioning,' said Parker. 'That could have had something to do with it.'

Flint was watching the behaviour of the other sheriff and Parker's men closely, determined he was not going to miss a single second of what was going on. Parker merely lifted his chin and gave the slightest of nods; if Flint had not been watching both men with narrowed eyes he might even have missed it.

'OK, I'm in charge here.' Couhard looked at Flint, still holding a gun to his ribs. 'Joe, I'm willing to overlook this behaviour one more time, but you've proved that you ain't fit to be around here. Now, you're a free man, but it looks to me as if your way of setting about what you're doing has riled a few good citizens.'

'I ain't going to argue with you,' said Flint, keeping very still.

'It seems to me that you have no choice but to get out of town or you're risking getting your blamed head blown clean off your shoulders. Get on your horse, Flint, you're leaving in disgrace right now.'

Couhard did not turn to look at Parker or the men who were obviously working for him but, along with the crowd who had gathered, they were watching as Couhard got on his own mount, which was tethered so conveniently near by, ready to run the visitor out of town. Yet Flint sensed that the sheriff was doing just as he had been asked.

They rode to the edge of town wordlessly, the only sounds were those of their horses' hoofs and of the travellers coming in and out of the town across the busy trail. Flint stopped as they arrived at the Quinn spread.

'I have a few more questions I really should be asking,' he said.

' 'Tain't up for grabs,' said Couhard. 'I'll do any investigatin' that needs doing and send one of my men to tell you what gives, Joe.'

'Sure you will,' said Flint, unable to keep a slight trace of sarcasm out of his tone.

'Flint, you get out of here. I could shoot you like a rabid cur and most of the town wouldn't bat an eyelid. Now, I've taken your bullets; I suggest you ride for Greenville as fast as you can and we'll meet another day when all this has blown over. Get going.'

Flint did not answer but turned his steed back to the main road and urged Traveller onwards. He did not say goodbye because inside his head he could not help thinking about an infant who might lose his poor mother and a man who lay dead and was to be buried in an anonymous grave.

As he rode away, bruised and weary, with the lump on the back of his head throbbing like hell, Flint knew that he wasn't saying goodbye to Afton at all.

CHAPTER NINE

Katie-Joe heard the sound of the window opening. There was a good reason for this, because Katie-Jo was sleeping in the small infirmary; three of the beds were empty, while Hank, the small boy, was lying beside her on the fourth.

There was also a good reason why she was here. Sister Theresa had told her that their patient – they still hadn't managed to get her name – was starting to have waking episodes. It might help her to have someone at her side with the baby that was obviously hers.

They had tried the experiment earlier on, when the young woman had woken and seen the child. For the first time she had smiled, had even managed to hold him in her arms, crooning a little as she did so, before going into that strange coma that overcame her each time she seemed to be recovering. Katie-Jo had been greatly moved by the episode.

'Will you stay?' asked Sister Theresa. 'If you are

here with the child and she awakens for good I want you to be ready. Trust me, I know how strong the bond is between mother and child, I've seen it a thousand times in my life.'

With a plea like that Katie-Jo could not resist staying to do as she was asked. What were a couple of nights of discomfort if they led to the young woman's recovery? Nothing, that was what.

There had been one more instance of the young woman waking in the early evening and again Katie-Jo had taken the child to her, holding him so tightly that he wriggled and squirmed to get away, but even this had not wiped the beatific smile off the woman's face as she once more slipped into deep sleep.

Katie-Jo and Hank had eaten in the refectory with the sisters, who had made a huge fuss of him which he had thoroughly enjoyed.

'But what about the children?' asked Katie-Jo as she was shown her bed in the side room, thinking of school the next day.

'That has been taken care of,' said Sister Theresa with a little smile. 'I will stand in for you.'

'You will?'

'Oh yes. Well, I taught there for many years; it was my pleasure until the work with the mission increased.' Sister Theresa was full of surprises.

Now it was late at night, or early in the morning depending on how you looked at these things, and Katie-Jo was finding out that noises that you barely hear during the day can sound quite thunderous in the early hours.

Lying there, with the thumping of her heart threatening to drown out the sounds in the next room, Katie-Jo heard the catch of the window rattling, and decided that now was the time to make a move. She stood up in her bare feet, snatched up the brass candlestick at the side of the bed, and moved swiftly through to the annexe just as the window was being opened. There was a full moon outside, so by standing in the shadow of the doorway she was able to see the shadowy figure crawling over the sill and into the room. His knife glinted in the moonlight and as she waited – for what? – another weapon appeared in his other hand: a lead cosh.

She thought of the young man who had been trying to get into the room the other day. It was obvious now that his intentions had never been good in any respect. The man was obviously concentrating entirely on what he was doing as he moved towards the supine form of the injured woman. One slash of his knife, one blow of his cosh was all it would take, then whatever threat she posed to him would be gone for good.

Katie-Jo came forward noiselessly on her bare feet and, wielding the candlestick like a club, brought it down on the head of the man who was apparently trying to kill the young woman. He whirled around and lashed at Katie-Jo with the knife, but she brought down the candlestick again and he dropped to the ground with a reassuring thud. It was the first time she had ever hit someone in real anger.

There was a shuffling of footsteps as the sisters

approached, having heard sounds of the commotion coming from the room. Sister Theresa entered bearing an oil lamp that cast an eerie glow on the proceedings. Her mouth was a grim line as she looked at the man on the ground, the cosh and the knife lying beside his prone body telling their own story.

'How are you?' she asked Katie-Jo. The school-teacher shook her head.

'Never mind me,' she said, 'we should have stopped him earlier when we had the chance.' She turned the man over, expecting to see the smooth face of the young cowboy who had been trying to kill the young mother; instead she found that she was looking into the coarse, unshaven face of an older man whom none of them had seen before.

The sisters, who were used to manual labour from tending their crops and drawing water from the well, dragged the stranger outside and set him down in the courtyard.

'We'll lock him up,' said Katie-Jo. 'Joe gave me the keys to his office, just so that there would be someone who could use them if trouble started and we needed to get in. I never thought I might *have* to use them.'

On the borders of a place like Greenville there was always some kind of movement. Seeing the light of their oil-lamp a tall figure, spare of build but with broad shoulders, came stepping over to them.

'Can I help you, ladies?'

It was the young man whom Katie-Jo had suspected of being the would-be killer. She did not question him too closely but looked down at the man on the ground.

'Yes,' she answered, 'you can help us take this miscreant to jail to have him locked up.'

Ty might have been young but he was strong. He picked up the prone body and carried him across to the sheriff's office, where Katie-Jo opened up and lighted an oil lamp that hung from the ceiling. Ty set the man down on a cot in one of the open cells.

'Looks like he's got a head wound,' he grunted, leaning over the body. 'Doesn't look as if it's bleeding too bad.'

'Then leave him be,' said Katie, who had unhooked the keys to the three cells that were situated behind the sheriff's office. She tried them until she found the right one, then clanged the door shut and locked it firmly. The young man turned to her.

'Does this have anything to do with that young woman – what's her name? – whom you have over there?'

'Yes it does; he was trying to kill her.'

'Was he!'

Katie-Jo saw a flash of real anger; for a moment she felt afraid because the man's youthful features were contorted with fury. Then she saw that the anger was not directed at her.

'That rattlesnake! I oughta go back into that cell there and finish the job you started. . . Miss. . . ?'

'Katie-Jo.'

'Ty is my name. I never heard anything so low in my life.' The young man's anger seemed so genuine that she was left in no doubt at all: he was rallying to the defence of an innocent, helpless woman.

'I guess I got off on the wrong foot with you the other day,' he said humbly. 'I just wanted to go and see the woman who had been injured, to see if I knew her. I'm afraid I gave the wrong impression.'

'Come to think of it,' said Katie-Jo, 'how is it that you are up and about this early in the morning?'

'I guess I couldn't sleep for thinking about what had happened,' Ty said, 'and some bars around here are open all night. Guess I was going to get a skinful and try to get some sleep that way. So,' he said, shifting tack, 'who's in charge of the kid?'

'I am,' Katie-Jo replied. 'Talking of that, it's time I went back to the mission. The sisters are looking after the child – they've called him Hank – but he'll be wondering where I am; he's used to me,' she added.

'You're fond of that kid,' said the stranger. 'I can hear it in your voice. Say, would you let me come over later, and just see the kid and the woman for five minutes?'

'The woman was on the verge of dying a couple of days ago,' said the schoolteacher. 'I'm sure that the reason she seems to be the road to recovery so quickly is because I'm there with Hank. I suppose it's not too much to ask someone to wait patiently, for a couple more days until she's awake, talking for herself and would maybe like a visitor or two?'

'I guess.' He did not try to argue the point, seeing that she was making a concession towards him.

'Why do you need to see her so urgently anyway, Ty?'

'Just to get a few things straight in my head, that's all. But I can't explain why, not right now.'

'I think I misjudged you,' Katie-Jo said, looking at him with her head tilted a little to one side. 'Well, I'd better get this place locked up; Joe should be back later today. I'm going back to the mission to look after Hank – and get some sleep.'

'Tell you what: I'll stay here, brew a coffee and guard this miscreant until your sheriff comes back,' said Ty.

Katie-Jo looked at him long and hard.

'I'll trust you. But watch out if you're up to some double cross.'

'So is your sheriff mean enough to do something real bad to me?'

'He is, and so is Sister Theresa, I wouldn't cross her in a million years.'

CHAPTER TEN

When Joe Flint reached town, battered and bruised though he was, the first place he went to was the home of his friend the schoolma'am. He was startled to find that she was not there; however, her fellow teacher directed him to the Order of St Xavier's mission, where he found that she was looking after Hank. When the infant saw who had arrived a big grin spread all over his cherubic face. He held out his arms and kicked his legs as if he was trying to air-walk towards Flint, much to the consternation of Katie-Jo, who was holding him at the time.

'Hello, big guy,' said Flint, sweeping up the child even though a sharp pain jerked through his body at the effort. He was going to look well-bruised on arms and neck in a few hours. He smiled and talked a few nonsense words with Hank for a minute or two, much to the infant's delight, then he turned to the girl.

'You look wonderful, Katie-Jo; motherhood would suit you.'

'I must say, Flint, that you look like hell, as if you'd been dragged behind your horse.'

'Worse than that. I've been set about by a bunch of no-gooders and stymied in my mission. Still, that's a tale for another day. What's been happening around here?'

'Nothing much, except that they tried to murder Hank's mother.'

'They? Who are "they"?'

'I don't really know who has been up to what, Joe, but I think you'll be interested in what – or rather *whom* – I have to show you in the jailhouse.'

Katie-Jo left Hank in charge of one of the sisters and, with Flint leading the way, they went along the road and up to his office. It was already well past midday and the streets were bustling with traders, cowboys on business and women going about their everyday concerns. He did not ask her for any details on the way over. The way he felt right now made him long for a hot bath and a good meal, followed by a long rest, but that wasn't the way of the world; he had work to do.

He was startled to find that his office was now occupied by a tall, lithe man sitting in the pinewood chair. The stranger had his feet up on the desk, his hat over his face and was snoring fit to bust. Ty, it seemed, had finally succumbed to his lack of sleep the previous night.

'Hey!' said Flint.

The man awoke with a jerk, pulled himself to his feet and grabbed for his gun. He gave a fleeting grin as he looked at Flint.

'I guess you must be the sheriff,' he said. 'Your little lady there recruited me as a kind of unofficial deputy. Ty's the name, Ty Cooder.'

'Ty has an interest in our case,' said Katie-Jo, 'and he was awfully good last night. Helped me out with that vile criminal.'

Flint walked through his office to the cells and peered into the end cell on the left. The man who lay there was unshaven, looking as if he too had been having a hard time of it with clothes that were dusty and torn in one or two places. He seemed to be about the same height as Flint, but more thickset; the wound on his head was clearly visible through his thinning hair.

'Your handiwork?' he asked Ty.

'Nope, the young lady here did a fine job of laying this one out,' said Ty.

The man on the cot in the cell opened his eyes, groaned and sat up. He looked at Flint through heavy-lidded eyes. His voice came out as a low rasp.

'Sheriff, you've got to let me go. All this is a mistake. Let me go now.'

'What's your name?'

'Look, I can't remember a thing, got a bad blow to the head. Sheriff, I need to see the doc.'

'Wait a minute.' Flint tilted his head to one side. 'I know your face from somewhere. What's your name? That's all I need to know.' The prisoner did not answer this question but struggled to his feet, tottered forward and rattled the bars.

'Let me out. I swear it ain't my fault.'

'Shut up,' said Flint. 'I'll listen to your side in a minute. Katie-Jo, let's get out of here. Have you fed the prisoner, Ty?'

'Yep, he was awake at seven this morning. I shared a pot of coffee with him and fed him bread and beef jerky. He's doing fine in that department.'

The three of them went back to the office. Flint took back his keys from Katie-Jo and as they stepped outside he could hear the man bellowing.

'He'll be safe until I come back,' he said as he locked up.

By unspoken consent the three of them drifted off to Mama's Eatery, which was little more than a glorified log cabin, but where Flint knew the food cooked by Conchita was some of the best you could get this side of the border. This was where they were able to partake of fare that included *fajitas* filled with spicy beef and drink copious amounts of coffee. When they were finished the two men rolled their cigarettes, sat smoking and listened to the tale that Katie-Jo had to tell.

Flint was feeling more relaxed than he had been for many hours. He looked at the schoolteacher as she finished.

'So you say he kind of lurched forward as he walked?'

'Yes. I think he's injured one of his legs in some way. Why do you ask?'

'Just working on some idea in the back of my head, that's all.' He turned his attention to the younger man. 'So what's your story? Why do you want to see the woman who was injured?'

'I just want to find out if she's who I think she is, is all.'

'Which kind of leads to the question of who do you think she is?'

'I'm not really sure of that; I only think that she might be Emily.'

'Emily who?'

'Sheriff, sometimes things ain't as cut and dried as you think they are. I don't even know some of the most basic answers, and I ain't the type to speculate until I do.'

'Well, if that's how you work, it's laudable enough, I guess. Just hope you're not making any plans to get away soon, because you might be needed.'

'I'll stay a few more nights; got plenty of money, I guess. I haven't been able to go out gambling and roistering like I planned, not with this on my mind.'

'Well, you two do as you want.' Flint stood up and jammed his hat on his head. 'I have me a prisoner to interrogate.'

He was out of the door before they could answer. Somehow he trusted Ty with Katie-Jo, despite that young man's evasiveness.

The prisoner sat in his cell, hunched over, looking a picture of misery. He glared at Flint as the sheriff entered the office.

'I need you to talk, mister,' said Flint. 'I want to know why you broke into an infirmary and tried to cut the throat of an innocent woman.'

'Get to hell!' said the man behind the bars. The prisoner had obviously decided, on reflection, that the best way he could deal with his incarceration was by not cooperating with the law.

'Well, see, I reckon hell is reserved for no-good cut-throats,' said Flint. 'What were you doing there? Why did you want to kill her?'

The man did not respond.

'See, I've been thinking about that,' said Flint, 'and I don't reckon you bear that much of a personal grudge.'

Still no response. This did not trouble Flint in the least; he was used to people trying to stymie him, and in this situation *he* was not the one under attack.

'Go to hell!' said the prisoner again, underlining the point by bringing up a gobbet of phlegm and spitting it in Flint's direction. 'I got friends. Once the word's out I won't be here long.'

'So who are your friends?' asked Flint.

'You'll see.' The man turned away and lay down again on his bed, back turned towards the sheriff. Flint knew he was perfectly within his rights to drag the man out and cut up rough with him. He knew, however, that the pressure on a man's mind is a surer way of getting information out of him than a physical beating. Also, he had not come back to speak to the prisoner totally unprepared. He produced one of the Wanted posters, which he'd taken from those that had been lying on his desk since a few days before.

'Funny; we get these things that they print in Santa

Fe sent out to us along with the mail,' he said. 'I guess most of these here miscreants won't be coming near Greenville. Take Gil Beemis, for instance; if I could prove that he was around here I could get a good reward for him.'

Was it his imagination or had the man quivered slightly, even though he did not turn round?

'I'll tell you what I think happened, shall I? Then maybe we'll see if we can get together and discuss your future, Beemis.' The man still did not turn round, but his breathing was shallow, not indicative of one who is resting.

'I'll tell you what happened. You didn't do any of this on your own. For some reason you were paid to go and intercept a coach that was on the road to Greenville.'

The man still did not turn round but his breathing remained shallow. Flint knew that he had caught the man's attention.

'You said something that made the driver stop. What was his name, by the way? "Jack" or good old "George" or something like that? Anyway, you knew his name, didn't you? He was getting ready to go and you showed him you weren't toting a gun. You probably had it tucked into the back of your belt.' He could picture the scene unrolling in his head.

'You were halfway between Afton and Greenville by then. The road is rough as all get-out, real rutted and uneven. You got off your horse and you went over to the coach and the woman put her head out – foolishly as it turns out, but she's young and young persons can be foolish and too trusting – and you coshed her on the head. She fell back and you were going to grab the infant – for whatever reasons of your own. Then the coachman recovered his wits. Good old George cracks the whip and the next thing you know the coach is rolling away – mother, infant and all.'

He paused and looked towards where the prisoner lay, twitching a little as if he were pretending to be asleep, but in reality he was alert to what was being said.

'You turned and went towards your horse to give chase, but you weren't the only thing that turned. The ground beneath was all rutted – I saw it myself just hours ago – and you went over on your ankle, busting it completely. Even then, as you lay there, you pulled out your gun and took a few pot shots at the departing coach. You thought you'd missed, didn't you? Because it kept on rolling.'

He was still getting no direct response but he heard a low groan from the prisoner and knew that he was following the right trail.

'You were hired, weren't you? You knew that you would get paid by results, so you lay there for long enough, collapsed on the ground with your injured ankle, until you were able to master the pain and get on your mustang. You rode into town and put yourself up at the seediest hotel – The Grand – and you lay there for a couple of days because your broken ankle meant that you were in no fit state to continue. By the third night you'd strapped up your leg and you went out and that's when you went after the young woman. Everyone in town knew what happened to her, so it wasn't hard for you to find out where she was.'

He paused for quite a while then to let the thoughts sink into the brain of the man, who still lay there without reacting.

'I'll tell you what I'll do, Beemis. I'll get you back to face the charges of bank robbery and maybe I'll even manage to get your sentence commuted – if you cooperate with the law. I know what you are, Beemis; you're a brute without much in the way of human feeling. You would have slit the throat of the woman after coshing her without a second's thought, grabbed the child and killed him, then you would have gone back for your reward.'

Was it his imagination or did the man in the cell show signs of stirring? Flint was relentless as he continued:

'But I know men like you: you want to live, and that's the chance I'm giving you. Tell me why this happened and I'll at least help you escape from the hangman's noose.'

There came a creaking sound as the wooden bed strained under the prisoner's not inconsiderable weight. He swung his legs over the side and looked at Flint with red-rimmed eyes. The two men stared silently at one another, sizing up the moment. Flint did not let any emotion show on his rugged features because he knew that such subtle signs could tip an interrogated man one way or the other.

'I ain't blabbing,' said Beemis. 'You got no idea.' This might have seemed a negative response, but Flint saw it as an encouraging sign.

'Talk to me,' he said, 'and I'll get you out of here right away and you'll get a fair trial in Santa Fe. Believe it or not, they'll take your honesty into account.' He looked Beemis in the eye, then glanced at the big old clock on the wall.

'Guess it's time to give you some food.'

He gave the prisoner bread, cheese and some hot coffee. Beemis looked suprised but Flint knew what he was doing. He had made the man an offer, he had relaxed the man, now he was giving the man time to think. It was a much better way of softening up thugs like Beemis – if indeed Beemis was the thug and he was pretty sure he was – who reacted to violence with more violence. 'I have to go now, but maybe we can have a little chat about your prospects when I come back in half an hour.' He walked towards the door Beemis said nothing, but there was a light in his eyes that suggested he would be ready to talk when the sheriff returned.

Katie-Jo was in the mission when Flint got there. There was a look in her eyes such as he had barely seen on their last few meetings: a look of suppressed excitement and joy.

'Where's that cowboy?' he asked, thinking that perhaps she had let him in to see the injured woman against all instructions, that she might have something to tell him in that regard.

'Ty? He's gone back to his hotel as far as I know. He's being patient because he knows how bad she's been. That isn't what I was going to tell you.'

'What then?'

'I took Hank in to see her. This time when she woke up she was a lot stronger. She held him for a long time, stroked his head and let him pat her cheeks. Then I called her "Emily" and she nearly jerked her head off her neck looking at me. I asked her if her name *was* Emily.'

'She said "yes"?' enquired the sheriff.

'No. In fact she looked a little scared, and then a look of great weariness passed over her. She gave Hank back to me and sank down into an even deeper sleep.'

'I'm confused now,' said Flint. 'Why should we be worried if she didn't say "yes"?'

Hank had been playing with a carved wooden train on the floor. He crowed with delight when he saw Flint, who picked him up, giving a little grunt as he did so.

'I swear this woman is feeding you on more rocks than ever. You get heavier every time I lift you.' Hank chuckled at this and tried to thwack the sheriff on the head with the little train.

'Hey, watch it, laddie!' Flint protested.

'You don't understand. I think she recognized her own name, but she's still only half-remembering what happened to her. She'll be up and about in no time.'

'That is good news; the sooner she can talk about what happened the sooner we might clear up at least some of this mess. Well, now that I know mother and baby are doing well I'm going back over to see the prisoner.'

'Did you rough-house him?'

'Hell, no, he's about the same height as me but he's a bull of a man. I don't tackle that kind unless I've really got the upper hand. No, I played on his mind.'

'Good, that's the best way. I hope they hang the bastard. Put down that baby.'

Flint obeyed. Katie-Jo looked at him with such shining eyes that he could make no other response but to take her in his arms. He kissed her for what seemed like seconds but was really a minute or so, her warm body sparking thoughts of how things might be between them one day.

'Get him,' she said. She let him go, but there seemed to be a deep promise in the look she exchanged with him.

Flint sauntered to the outside of the mission where he had a long slow, smoke. As he stood there he saw a horseman in a dark cloak riding past on a quarter horse at a good lick. This garb was not as unusual as might be thought; it was early evening now and a cloak would keep a rider warm and the grit out of his face if he was journeying over rough ground. It was rather the fact that the rider already had his face covered and was going at a good speed that attracted his attention.

He threw away the remains of his smoke, turned

the corner and walked slowly over to his office. He unlocked the door and went inside. The door leading to the cells was open and Flint could see that Beemis was sprawled against the door of his cell. Flint's first thought was that the prisoner had experienced some kind of heart attack. When someone was under this kind of extreme stress that could happen quite easily. But as he came closer he saw the blood in the twilit cell: blood that pooled on the ground between the man's legs.

Cursing loudly Flint got his keys and unlocked the door of the cell. Beemis fell sprawling out on to his back as door opened. The front of the prisoner's shirt was soaked in his blood.

Beemis had suffered from heart failure all right, mainly because of the short-handled knife that was sticking out from the middle of his chest.

CHAPTER ELEVEN

Ty was in the hotel brooding moodily over his options. He had been here for a few days now. As far as time was concerned he could meet up with his fellow cowprods and go back on the trail. Every additional day he spend here now meant that he was losing money. Yet strangely, the thought no longer bothered him. He had learned that curiosity was a driving force that would keep him here until he had the answers that he wanted.

There came the sound of a heavy fist pounding on the door of his room. He opened up to find Sheriff Flint standing there.

'Where have you been?' asked Flint. The cowboy nodded to indicate the bottle of whiskey and the glass at the side of the bed.

'Here,' he said, 'just waiting, for what I don't know.'

'Did you come straight here?'

'I guess.'

Flint looked at the younger man long and hard.

'So you didn't go near the jailhouse?'

'Nope, you're the one who was softening up the prisoner.'

'Ty, I'm going to trust you. You're a cowboy and you know how to ride. I want you to do a little job for me. We'll do it together.'

'Guess you'd better tell me all about what you need me to do, then.'

'You don't seem that surprised.'

'Sheriff, when you've been out on the trail nothing surprises you. I've been run at by bulls bigger'n a shack and I've been near trampled to death in a stampede of beeves panicked by a few gunshots going off, not to mention being near drowned in the Red River, the Cimaroon and the Colorado – to name but three.'

'Well, I've got me a problem. Our prisoner decided after a little persuasion that he didn't want to get his neck burned by a noose. I left him to think the matter over, as you do.'

'That sure doesn't sound like a problem to me. Sounds as if you're getting what you wanted.'

'Sure, but when I came back the prisoner was letting in air around a dagger embedded in the middle of his chest, and letting out a lot of blood. He's in the morgue now. Guess old Lawrie will be delighted; the territory has to pick up the bill and that's two jobs in three days.'

'What happened?'

'My guess is that whoever hired him learned that Beemis – I'm assuming that's who the prisoner was –

had been captured. They knew that he was a pretty tough guy or they wouldn't have hired him for the job, but they also knew that they couldn't take any chances on him talking.'

'But how could they get to him? He was locked in a cell behind your office.'

'Probably a lot more easily than you think. I'm guessing that whoever did this hung about until he saw me coming over to the mission's infirmary to check out the injured woman, leaving the prisoner to stew on his own, unguarded.'

'He might have had to wait for hours.'

'Maybe, but maybe it was worth the wait. I guess that after I was gone he stood on something – a barrel or a box out back – and shouted out to Beemis. Beemis stood on his wooden bed, looked out of the window, saw the feller – who was no stranger to him – and asked him if he'd come to help him.'

'You don't know all this for a fact, Sheriff.'

'The feller – whom Beemis knew as the man who had hired him – said he *would* help, and he instructed Beemis to get as close to the window as he could. When the prisoner came up to the window the feller pushed forward, grabbed him by the hair and stuck the knife right into him. Beemis staggered backwards and hit his head against the iron bars of his cell. For him that was the end.'

'I guess you've got it all worked out, then?'

'Not really. I saw a horseman in a mighty hurry to get out of town earlier on today. After finding the body I could have ridden off after him, but instead I came here to check you out.'

'Why?'

'I didn't just come up here to talk to you; I've already seen Ramon and he confirmed that you haven't moved since coming back here. Your horse is still at the livery, too; I found that out as well.'

'Thanks for being so trusting, Sheriff.'

'Katie-Jo's the trusting one. I wouldn't have left you alone with the prisoner last night. Sure, you had your story for being out late, but perhaps you were Beemis's accomplice and that's the reason you were showing such an interest in the injured woman.'

'I wasn't anyone's accomplice.' The young man saw that Flint was looking at him closely and his face coloured. 'I guess I can tell you a little story, Sheriff. A man's been on the trail – say, less than two years ago – and he comes into a town like Greenville after delivering a whole lot of beeves to the Indian reservation.'

'I guess that could happen.'

'Like a lot of the cowboys he's been starved of female company for a long time. He comes into town and finds out there's a dance on a Saturday night.'

'Still sounds like the kind of thing that could happen.'

'Supposing that at the dance a guy meets a girl who waltzes with him and she's real soft and pretty, and later, when her grandfather, who's come there with her, gets distracted by business, she decides to go out for a breath of fresh air with that guy?'

'I can see that their meeting might lead to a few

complications,' said Flint thoughtfully.

'And suppose that they're both filled with the joys of spring that you get when you're real young and you can't help it, but you want to do the things that come naturally in a nearby barn where the hay is soft and the music's drifting over from the dance next door. . . ?'

'What could be more natural?'

'Say, are you taking the roast, friend?' The young man paused in his narration and glared at the sheriff.

'If anything I'm jealous, cowboy. That's my story you're telling.'

'Well, after we . . . after we got to know each other that way, she ran away real fast and a good thing too, because her grandfather comes out looking for her with a gun in his hand and she just tells him I've lighted out of there. He rides off with her in a green coach and that's the last I see of Emily.'

It was early evening by then. In this part of the world the shades of night grew fast. Flint looked at the young man and realized that Ty knew very little about the situation if he was telling the truth, and telling the truth was what he seemed to be doing.

'You'll be able to do what you want, Ty, if you help me out. The injured woman is getting stronger all the time, but I need you to help me.'

'I'm listening.'

First thing in the morning a bleary-eyed sheriff rode around to El Gran Hotel. In a town where people got up at an unearthly hour to work in the mines, or to travel over the border, he was still early. The dawn light was a distant promise on the skyline and there were only the few lights left burning in the street to illuminate his way.

Ty was standing outside the hotel with his horse, Juke, distinguished by its white socks and a white blaze on its forehead. He too seemed a little worse for wear, but then he had been drinking the night before and had sat up half the night just thinking about what he was going to do this day. He threw the remains of his cigar away as Flint arrived and the two of them set off across the open country.

Neither of them spoke much, Ty letting the older man set the pace. They rode steadily across the rough countryside as the light gradually began to seep across the vast sky; as the blood began to course through their veins both men felt better, ready for what was to come. One or two riders passed them during that time: travellers who had business of their own in the ranches that surrounded the towns.

Eventually they halted at the outskirts of Afton, beside the smart municipal sign announcing the name of that town. The shadowy bulk of a grand mansion lay to their right; there was a stand of sycamore trees to their left. There was no sign of a light in the large building, but by then they were in a kind of twilight that would last for at least another half-hour.

'You know what we have to do?' said Flint. He was about to commit burglary for the first time in his life.

Strangely enough the thought did not bother him in the least because he was about to solve a great mystery.

'What are we trying to do?' asked Ty as they led the horses under the shelter of the trees and tied them to a convenient low-hanging branch.

'It's as simple as this: the last time I was here the meeting was being controlled by two people with outside interests. We're going to go into the house, see Mr Quinn and have a little private talk with him. He can cry foul next time he sees that annoying partner of his, but by that time I'll have some evidence to bring to bear.'

Ty cocked a glance at Flint as they crossed the road.

'This ain't just a search for you, is it? It's personal, ain't it?'

'About as personal as you can get. Now hush up, son, because we've a stiff task ahead of us.'

Ty held his tongue as he was asked and the two men went round to the side of the mansion. Both of them were armed: Ty with an old Colt .32 he had picked up somewhere along the trail; it was loaded, but he had only a few spare bullets in his pocket. Flint had his Colt .44 secured in a leather holster at his side. It too was loaded; he had learned a lesson from his last trip to Afton. He also wore a bullet belt, showing he really wasn't taking any chances.

They managed to get in through a side window, levering it up with a metal instrument that Flint had brought with him especially for that purpose, and within seconds they were inside the building itself. Inside it was a great deal darker than it was outside; Flint held up a hand to keep Ty from moving forward along the passageway in which they found themselves. Something was niggling at the back of his mind. He had not decided to bring his weapon with him merely as a precaution in case of any unpleasantness from Quinn or Parker: big houses like this had servants and dogs, though so far he had heard neither.

After a little while, when their eyes had grown accustomed to the lower light level inside the house, Flint urged Ty to keep behind him as they moved forward together. He needed a second man with him to provide back-up while he was questioning old man Quinn. Together they climbed the wide stairs that led up to what must be the master bedroom. When they reached the landing they both had their guns in their hands, ready to face down whoever might appear.

Flint threw the bedroom door wide open and stepped inside. There was a luxurious four-poster bed, such as a man of Quinn's status might enjoy, but it was completely undisturbed as if it had not been slept in for a long time. They both stood in the doorway, holding their guns and looking round. The sound of emptiness as they walked down the stairs told Flint all he needed to know.

The Quinn mansion was unoccupied and had been for a long time.

CHAPTER TWELVE

'Guess there's not a lot we can do,' said Ty. 'That sure was a let-down.'

Flint looked sideways at the young man and realized that here was a person who was used to action, had come here in the expectation of finding a way of releasing his youthful energy, might even have been anticipating a fight.

'Just be glad that nothing happened,' he said. 'Still, this is mighty strange. Come on, let's look out back. I don't think the hounds're gonna be nipping our heels any time soon.'

At the back of the mansion, which they arrived at by climbing out of a back-room window to circumvent the wooden fence and the locked gate that would have otherwise barred them, they found a wide expanse of grass dotted with palmetto trees and with a fountain in the middle. The stable block was to one side and there was an annexe leading off from the main house that was obviously the servants' quarters.

'All locked and sealed,' said Flint. 'You can get away with a lot when a place is sealed up like this.' They came to the edge of the grass, near the stables, where flowerbeds had been dug in the past. Evidently the old man had enjoyed looking out of his windows to see tall sunflowers brightening up the view, but these were all dead now and going to seed. One of the flowerbeds, however, had been freshly dug over.

'Look at all this space for growing,' said Ty, 'and not even one 'tater planted. This place is near as big as the farm-holding my parents have back in Utah.'

'Never mind what rich folks have,' said Flint who had been around too long to be impressed by the trappings of wealth. 'Look at this; looks to me as if someone's been caretaking this place and they've decided to do some digging as part of their duties.'

'What are you saying?'

'Guess that a man might be more useful in the minds of some people if he's alive,' said Flint, 'because if he's alive then certain things don't need to be dealt with in law.'

Ty looked slightly baffled at this. He was a straight-forward cowpuncher, living in a world where high-flown thoughts and details were left at the road-side.

'I think it's time we went back inside and did a bit of searching,' said Flint.

'Exactly what are we looking for?' Ty still looked baffled. This made Flint scratch his head a little.

'You know what? It's something that I'll know I've

111

been searching for when I find it.' With these enigmatic words Flint climbed back into the house through the window.

They were not burglars in the usual sense. The valuables they were seeking would yield not money but knowledge; Flint was fairly certain that Quinn would have been a fairly traditional businessman, so one of the things he tackled was a roll-top bureau that he found in the front room where he had met the old man. He lost no time in inserting the blade of his knife into the catch and twisting upwards so that the lock gave way.

Ty, still in a state of puzzlement, looked on while his companion was doing this. Flint looked inside the desk and found various items: pads for writing on, a blotter, pens, ink and a pile of papers. He took out the papers and sifted through them one by one. When he was halfway through he paused and extracted a document that looked more official than the rest, most of which were letters.

The piece of paper in his hand was a large, yellowed manuscript, covered in spidery writing in black ink. Some of the writing seemed much fresher than the rest; the words scrawled at the top, however, were stark enough:

Last Will and Testament.

Ty, peering over Flint's shoulder, looked slightly startled as he read this.

'How the heck did you know to look for that?'

'This isn't his final will,' said Flint, scanning the document rapidly. The crabbed writing was hard to make out, but he persisted. Most of it was about land, shares and property, so he skipped over those parts. 'What you're looking at is a draft document, not the final piece; that would have been passed on to his lawyers to be drawn up properly. Look at this.'

'I – I don't rightly know how to make it out,' said Ty. 'You give it a read.' It was clear that the young man was not well-lettered, a common thing among cowboys. Flint did not hold his lack of literacy against him; book-learning was not mandatory when chasing beeves.

'It says that he includes his granddaughter in his will and that she is to inherit the majority of the shares, this house and the land,' said Flint. 'But notice, the handwriting in this part is far worse than what's gone before. He was failing when he wrote this.'

He scanned the document even more closely and looked at some of the notes written in the margins.

'Something here about Madison's farm. Why would a man like Quinn be bothered about a farm? Looks to me as if there's a reason for a place like that being on his mind. And look, there's a mention of a housekeeper, and a manservant whom he also calls his groundskeeper: Mrs Parker and Frank Tulloch. Notice that the name "Parker" is a fairly recent addition. I'm guessing his daughter would have done that job when she was here.' He tucked the document into his breast pocket.

'What happened?' asked Ty.

'I guess we can all make up stories,' said Flint. 'Fact is that Nat Parker decided to carry out a little deception: a play just for me. I'm guessing he hired some old drunk from town to play the part of Quinn and they stage-managed the meeting for every second that I was here. They wanted me to believe it because they don't want anyone to know he's dead yet.'

He looked about them at the musty room. 'And I'm guessing that's why we don't have any pictures hanging around here. I've never met Quinn, so any photographs were removed to make sure I didn't compare the man in front of me with his picture.'

'So what are we going to do?' asked Ty.

'I say we make a two-pronged attack. You go into town and ask a few questions on my behalf, if you're up for the job. They'll be waiting for me in town, I guess, especially that crooked sheriff.'

'What crooked sheriff?'

'Ben Couhard. He's obviously in the pocket of Nat Parker, and he'll arrest me on sight if I come within as much as spitting distance of the saloons. What I want you to do is to go around and find out some information about our man and his partners, then get back to me. Try and get as much knowledge as you can find about Quinn, too.' Flint looked at the young man and Ty straightened up.

'You would trust me that much?'

'See, the way I see it, either you're with me or against me. If you're against me you've had countless opportunities to show your hand, and you haven't.

Either you're playing some kind of long game or you are exactly what you seem to be.'

'I'll do it,' said Ty. 'I guess I'll need some funds, though, if I'm going to bum around looking for information.'

'Don't worry, I have some money here.'

Flint did not mention the fact, but the coffers were getting low. He was given only so much money by the county to carry out his duties, and he was not that well paid either. However, he thought this might be a bad time to bring up that particular topic.

'The other thing is the young woman – call her Emily for now; everyone knows where she is. Now that she's getting better it wouldn't be too much of a stretch to get her away from the sisters, caring though they may be, and put her into some other kind of accommodation, even a bedroom in The Grand. If they want her dead that badly they're not going to rest until they've got what they want.'

'Maybe all this is for nothing,' said Ty. 'Remember, boss, I still haven't seen hide nor hair of the woman. She could still be a complete stranger.'

'Is it really for nothing, then? Wouldn't you like to help a young lady who just might die at the hands of a low-down slimy worm like Parker?'

'I guess,' said Ty, not looking entirely convinced by the argument. It was clear from the look on his face that a doubt had entered his mind. 'All right, I'll do it, but at the first sign of trouble I'm lighting out of there. I've got my own hide to consider.'

'Wouldn't expect it to be any other way. Now, let's

get out of this graveyard of a building.'

They had just reached the window through which they had originally entered the mansion when Flint pulled back and closed it so suddenly that he almost caught Ty's fingers.

'Did you hear that?'

'Hear what?'

But Ty needed no answer from Flint because the sound of horses' hoofs drumming over the dry ground of the road filled their ears. It was still early and, except for the ticking of the grandfather clock in the front room, there was not a sound to be heard in the house. This meant that noises from outside seemed unnaturally loud. The sound of the hoofs came closer; then, instead of continuing into the distance they rattled to a halt outside the mansion. There was a further sound of hoofbeats as one horse moved on into the distance, but another one clattered and neighed outside.

'Get down,' said Flint. He ran from the passage-way into a large room. He crawled over to the bay window at the front of the room. The window was heavily curtained – one of the reasons the room was so dark – and Flint crawled under the patterned fabric. He dared to raise his head above the sill. There, in front of the building, were three men whom he recognized immediately as his attackers from a couple of days before. They were all armed, and it was obvious from the way two moved out to either side, with one staying in the middle, that they intended to confront and kill the intruders who had dared to break into the home of Douglas Quinn.

Earlier that day Nat Parker looked grimly around at his men. He owned a ranch on the far side of Afton, and the three men, Jacobs, Coyle and Beeny were hired hands. When he had instructed them to take out the sheriff previously he thought that would be an end to the matter, but at least now they were useful for something. All three of the men were bleary-eyed, as he was too at this time of the morning. His mood wasn't too good either, since he was used to having a longer lie-in than most people in these parts.

'A little bird has told me that Sheriff Flint is investigating the home of an old friend,' he said. The 'little bird' referred to one of the riders who had passed the sheriff and Ty on their way out of Greenville. 'I want you boys to go there and make sure that neither of them emerges from there for quite a long time. Break a few windows and go inside if you want; just make sure you pin them down while trying to avoid getting yourselves killed. Think you can do that?'

'Sure we can,' said Coyle, the thickset man who had jumped on Flint's back the previous day. His soul was still smarting from the humiliation of being defeated by a shorter, slighter man and his legs still ached from the kicking he had received. 'Ain't that right, boys?'

The other two nodded a little less enthusiastically.

'Say, Mr Parker, are you coming to do this with us?' asked Coyle as they armed up with the weapons that Parker gave them. None of them habitually carried guns, given that they were mere ranch hands, but this had changed radically in the last few minutes. Another unusual feature of this enterprise was the fact that the men were going to be paid a huge bonus of two months' wages for getting out there and facing down the strangers. Parker knew what was at stake and he was not averse to paying his men well.

'No, I have other things to do,' said Parker, looking at them enigmatically. 'Let's put it like this: I'll be with you until a certain point, then I'll be leaving town altogether to do a little job.' He expanded no further on this matter.

True to his word Parker went out with them and saddled up his big Mexican horse with the rest. They rode out towards the big house. Parker found the two horses in the stand of sycamores. The horses would have been well enough concealed if no one had been actually looking for them.

'You get into position, boys; I have to get out of here now,' Parker told them. Then he rode off on his big brown gelding, the sound of the hoofs fading into the distance as his men got ready to bring down the intruders.

'All right for him to swan off and leave us to it,' said Coyle, who was not looking forward to their task.

'I don't think so,' said Beeny. 'I saw his face as he rode away and he was a man who looked worried, like real worried to death.'

'Whatever, let's do this.'

'Pin them down like the man said?'

'Nah. After what he did to us we're going to see to it that Sheriff Flint never gets back to his own town. Boys, you're going in to get him.'

CHAPTER THIRTEEN

When a man is faced with danger there are two things he can do. He can try and run away from that danger or he can face up to it and do the best he can.

Flint knew that he and Ty had the upper hand. They were inside the building, and that meant that the gunmen outside would have to try and get them out. On the other hand, because the gunmen were outside, this prevented Ty and Flint from getting to their horses and riding away from the scene of the attack. Even as he and his companion pulled aside the heavy drapes there was some movement from the greenery across the road.

'Come out with your hands up,' yelled Coyle. 'We'll make sure you get to the sheriff unharmed, and you'll face the right charges. If you don't come out we're coming in and you'll be taking your chances.'

'They're going to shoot us down in cold blood,' said Ty, who had been listening to these words.

'I don't think so,' said Flint. 'In fact I think if we

120

surrender they'll do exactly what they're saying and take us to be locked up by Couhard.'

'Then why attack us in the first place? Why didn't they just wait until we came out and attack us before we knew they were there?'

'That's a question,' said Flint thoughtfully. 'Seems as if they want to keep us pinned down as long as they can. That is what it looks like – and you keep an enemy pinned down for a reason.'

Both men had ducked down, one on either side of the bay window – luckily for them because there came the sound of a shot being fired. As soon as he heard the report Flint knew what it implied and he flung himself away from the window as quickly as possible. Ty, who was younger, with quicker reactions, but who had not reacted to the sound quite as swiftly just managed to get away as the bullet hit and the glass panes of the great window shivered into a million shards that sprayed into the room. Luckily the heavy drapes caught most of the blast.

Fortunately for the two men they had moved to either side, so they were shielded by the thick curtains and were little affected. If either of them had stayed where they had been they could have been badly cut by the jagged fragments of glass, which would have fallen on them like countless daggers.

'That's just a sample,' shouted Coyle. 'Now come out or we're coming in to get you.'

The two men in the room did not have to consult with each other; keeping low, and trying to avoid being cut by the glass that lay scattered everywhere, they made for the door of the room, which fortunately was still open. A couple of shots came from behind them as Coyle fired at their retreating forms. In seconds they reached the great hall. Flint seized an ornate chair with a red velvet seat, and thrust it in front of the door, then he ran up the stairs with Ty following closely behind him.

They had barely gained the second landing before they heard the sound of more breaking glass and loud curses as the men entered the building. Flint heard them talking to each other and surmised that only two of the attackers had come in to the house, the third being left outside to mop up anyone trying to escape.

Flint knew immediately what to do. It would be pointless to turn back and try fighting the men hand to hand because they would be keyed up and ready to fire at the first moving object they saw. He was not a coward, but did not see the point of being shot at if he could avoid it.

Instead he thrust Ty into the master bedroom and jumped in behind him. Fortunately there was a big iron key in the lock. Evidently Quinn had liked his privacy. Flint turned the key, hearing an audible *click*, then turned his attention to the window.

'We've got to deal with that gunman: he's holding us down while those two are after us.'

'We'll see about that, I guess,' said Ty grimly. There was a kind of concentrated fury about the young man that Flint had not seen in him before. Perhaps it was due to his getting sprayed with glass –

he had a few minor cuts on his face that were still wet with blood – or maybe it was the bullets that had zinged past his head when they were making their way out of the downstairs area, but Ty had a look that said he had taken enough of this behaviour, that he was going to stand up to the attackers.

He went over to the window, ducking down so that he was not an obvious target, stood to one side, wrapped his hat around his elbow and broke the lower window pane quickly and efficiently. As he pulled his arm away there came a round of gunfire from outside and bullets thudded into the window frame.

The problem was that it was hard to draw a bead on someone who was firing at you, so Ty was more or less forced to turn, take a pot shot in the general direction of the person aiming at him, then move away before he could be hit by returning fire.

Footsteps sounded on the stairs and two pairs of heavy boots thudded along the upstairs landing. Those outside had obviously sized up the fact that other doors were open and Flint saw the doorknob rattle as one of the two men tried to get into the master bedroom.

'Give up, feller,' yelled Jacobs from outside the room. 'This ain't a war, and it won't end good for you.'

'I think you might be wrong,' Flint called back. 'Give in now or you're a pair of dead men.'

The answer was a roar of gunfire as Beeny, outraged by this defiance, shot at the door. But the wood, being good solid oak did not give way and the bullet ricocheted in the confined space, causing Jacobs to utter a howl of fear.

'Dammit man! That nearly hit me when it bounced off. Coulda taken the top offa ma head and spilled ma brains.'

From inside the room Flint could not help thinking that in this case perhaps the gunman did not have a great deal of said cerebral matter to spill. There was no more in the way of warning, although he could hear them whispering to each other. It was frustrating being tied down here in this room, so Flint decided that he had to take immediate action.

Their whispered plan complete, he heard one of the men – probably Jacobs, who was the more solid of the two – retreating along the upper hallway. Then he heard the sound of rushing footsteps and the same hefty body thumped against the door. It was obvious what they were planning to do. When the door gave way the man bursting it open would fling himself to one side and his companion would blaze away with his weapon. It was a simple-minded attack plan, but one that had the merit of being direct, and might just succeed for that reason alone.

Flint decided to counteract the attempted breaking down of the door. He waited until he saw the doorframe quiver and crack as Jacobs thumped against the door for a second time and listened to the footsteps retreating along the hall. Then he unlocked the door, the click of the lock's mechanism being covered by the sound of heavy boots thudding along the passage. This time, instead of waiting for Jacobs to hurtle himself against the supposedly locked door, as the man was about to thump his shoulder against the wood Flint turned the doorknob and stepped to one side. As he did this there came another, less than shattering blow and Jacobs hurtled into the the room. Flint promptly cracked him on the back of the head with the butt of his Colt and the man fell to the ground like a stuffed gorilla.

This was not the end of the matter, for Flint booted the door closed with his foot and turned the key in the lock again. On the other side of the door Beeny gave a huge cry of rage and frustration and let loose a whole round of shots into the lock. The door swung slowly open, the lock now shattered, but in his anger Beeny had forgotten that when you empty a weapon you have to fill it again with bullets.

Flint swung the door wider open and held his Colt .44 level with Beeny's face.

'Hey partner, get inside, or I'll spill whatever little brains you were given across that polished floor,' he invited.

Beeny, turning white, threw up his hands and did as he was asked.

Meanwhile Nat Parker was making good time for Greenville. He did not ride as fast as he might in the slowy dawning light of day because he knew from what had happened to Beemis how easy it was to stumble and fall on a road like this. He wanted to get there in one piece.

For once in his well-planned life he did not know exactly what he was going to do. He thought of the building he had purchased long ago at the edge of Greenville. This was little more than a shack, made of wood and adobe like many others, bought as an investment for the land around it rather than the building itself because he thought there might be silver in the ground. He knew the cabin was still there, tucked into the green hills beside the river on the far edge of the town. He was the only person who knew that the cabin existed except for his sister and he was certain that she would not have told anyone a thing of such little consequence.

At his side he had a gun, a 0.32 Smith & Wesson, with extra bullets tucked in his pockets. Parker smiled a little coldly at this; he was a lawyer, a wheeler-dealer used to getting his way with words, but he could take action too, couldn't he? It would be no use shooting the girl down in cold blood in front of witnesses; even he couldn't get away with something like that, but he could make a strong case for getting her away.

He thought of the deposition tucked securely into his breast pocket. It was wonderful how a piece of paper could do what a gun couldn't.

He was cold but that would soon be remedied as the sun came over the horizon. He rode on with his face set into the semblance of a grin at the thought of what he was going to achieve in the next few hours.

Only it was a grin that would have made a small child scream for his mother.

That morning, even earlier, not far away, the young woman opened her eyes. This time when she got out of bed she walked around the room, albeit in a slow and rather tentative way, as if to reassure herself that she was now in full possession of her senses. That this was so was shown by the way her dark, liquid eyes took in the sparse decorations on the wall, the drawing of the man which hung across from the bed that had been her home for so long, and the bedside cabinet upon which sat the candle and the baby bottle from which the warm soup had been poured down her throat and into her waiting body.

She opened the door of the room. It was still early in the morning and the little building beyond was swathed in darkness. There was no one there. Vaguely she remembered there had been a woman here, with a baby.

'My baby,' she muttered, then said the words out loud a little louder. 'My baby. He's mine.' There was a sound behind her and she twisted around, almost losing her balance. Sister Theresa was standing there holding a lamp in her hand, still wearing her long night-robe.

'Bless you, child, I thought I heard you up even at this time of the day. You're just wandering around again. You're getting better all the time. I'll get you back to bed and you'll have some food soon. Perhaps your poor wondering brain will soon be as fit as your body; you are getting better in all ways.'

It was clear that she expected little from their unexpected guest. She came forward and took the young woman by the arm to lead her inside, as she had done so often before, but the woman pulled away from her and retreated a little into the shadows.

'Who are you? What am I doing here? What is this place? And where is my baby?'

Sister Theresa sat her lamp down and held out her hands for a second before pressing them together and looking up to what should have been the heavens but was really a smoky ceiling.

'Ah, the Lord be blessed, it's a miracle.' She remained like this for only a few seconds, her lips moving in silent prayer, then she put out her hands. 'You are restored, child. Come with me, we'll feed you, clothe you and help you get your strength back.'

Bewildered though she was, now that her senses had returned the woman responded to the kindness in the old sister's voice. Together they left the infirmary and went into the main body of the mission, the door of the infirmary closing behind the young woman for good.

It turned out that fine bedsheets, torn up, made perfectly respectable ropes and this was what Flint and Ty used them for with the two men, binding them and then tying them back to back on the ground.

'I have a feeling that we have to get out of here,' said Flint. 'You draw the fire of the one outside, and while you're doing that I'll get on his case.'

'I'll do that.' Ty went over to the window, once more ducking down to avoid being hit. He saw Flint run out of the room and heard him running down the steps as the acrid smell of gunpowder drifted to his nostrils from the shots fired earlier. Ty tried the same technique as before: stepping forward for a bare second and loosing a shot in the general direction of where the gunman might be.

This time he was not quite quick enough; for the first time he was caught by a bullet that tore through the lining of his jacket and hit him on the left shoulder. Luckily it had not gone in further down or it might have torn his arm half off. Even so the impact was enough to send him spinning across the room and he dropped his weapon. He cursed aloud a few times, then became aware of shouts from below. It seemed that Flint had managed to get outside.

Ty dared to look out of the window and saw the two gunmen confronting each other. Coyle was in some bushes; he had a sense of over-confidence because he had seen the young gunman upstairs shot down. He fired directly at Flint.

However the sheriff knew through long experience a couple of things that his opponent had not learned. The first was that it is far from easy to hit a moving target, especially one who is zigzagging expertly towards you; the second was that it is extremely intimidating to see a gun pointing straight at your face.

With wild imprecision Coyle, who would never have been a professional gunman, wavered and loosed a shot in the general direction of his antagonist. As is the way of these things, if he had tried he would not have succeeded, but he was lucky and the bullet caught Flint in one side, spinning him around precisely as another shot had done with Ty.

His gun went flying from his hand and he was just a few seconds from death as Coyle ran from the bushes to finish off his enemy, a grim expression on his face that showed he was not going to hesitate in doing so.

As he dashed forward there came a sudden crack from the upper window. Coyle froze like a statue and looked down. The bullet that had entered from behind had travelled down through his shoulder and exited through the right side of his chest. He gave a grunt of pain and surprise as the red droplets of blood spattered outwards, then he dropped to the ground face down.

Seconds later Ty was outside the building and at his friend's side, ignoring the other gunman altogether. Flint was still lying on the ground, but as he got to his feet with a helping hand he gave a grunt of agony, while Ty was still wincing at the pain in his shoulder.

'Just a graze,' said Flint, although his side was soaked with blood. 'Luckily it just parted the flesh. She'll be good as new in a coupla days. I'll bind her before we go.' They limped into the building together. Flint got Ty to help bind his wound with some of the cloth from the sheets, then they went back out and turned Coyle over. The man on the ground gave a groan. They stanched the bleeding from his wounds too.

'I'm done for,' he said, 'killed because of that bastard.' It was not clear to whom he was referring, but they had a feeling it was neither of them.

'No you ain't,' said Flint, 'you're wounded bad, but it missed your lungs. You ain't gonna die. Now spill the beans or you might find that you hit the heaven trail after all, spurred on by one sore and wounded sheriff, and one friend of his who's madder'n a wet hen.'

'Parker, he's going to get her.'

'Figured that much out. Where's he going to take her?'

'He has a place in the hills – near the silver mine. By the Doña Ana foothills.'

'How do you know?'

'I went out with his sister, she's . . . sweet on me. Told me about the place.'

'By the stars! I know that area – and the building,' said Flint. 'It's empty most of the time. Found it when we was out hunting. You better be telling the truth, boy.'

'I am,' came the reply, and from the pale and frightened face that looked back at them, they knew that he was.

At that moment a big man on a huge brown bay came riding towards them. He dismounted and had his gun in his hand before any of them could speak.

'You've done it now,' said Couhard. 'You're all under arrest.'

CHAPTER FOURTEEN

When Parker arrived in town he went straight to where he knew the woman was being kept: the Mission of St Xavier. He was dressed in riding trousers and had boots of Spanish leather that had been hand-made for him by a craftsman in Santa Fe; he could have been any one of hundreds of riders who passed through here in a year. But he was tall and square-set with a bearing that bore the unmistakable stamp of authority. Men of his type did not waste time thinking too deeply about what they were doing; in his eyes it was often the deed that counted.

His gun was at his side, ready to use if need be, as he thumped heavily on the peeling green paint of the mission door.

'Who is it?' asked a voice from the other side of the door.

'Ben Couhard,' said Parker, 'Sheriff of Afton. I'm here for a purpose.'

The door was not locked, it was normally left open for all who needed the care of the Sisters of St Xavier. Parker was not to know this. But soon he was confronted with a berobed lady, obviously well into her sixties, who regarded him with a jaundiced eye.

'I am Sister Theresa,' she said. 'How do I know you are who you say you are?'

'Ma'am, I'll make it easy for you. I am looking for a woman who has been involved in a serious case of murder.' As he spoke he pulled aside his waistcoat to show her the silver six-pointed badge pinned to his chest. The fact that he had had it made for him was neither here nor there because there was no possible way that she could know this. 'She would have had a baby with her. You would be taking care of the baby because the woman is an invalid.'

Sister Theresa stared at him for a few seconds that seemed to stretch into minutes for them both, then she gave a sigh and stood aside.

'All right, Sheriff – what did you say your name was?'

'Ben Couhard.'

'Well, Sheriff Couhard, you're making a mistake. There's no invalid here and no baby. But if you must come in you can do so.'

'I have a piece of paper here that says I can, by the judgment of the state.' He pulled out the deposition and waved it in her face.

'I don't need your piece of man-made rubbish,' said Sister Theresa. She turned and walked away with an agility that was surprising in a woman of her age.

Parker, having assumed the name of Couhard, ranged far and wide through the buildings. The mission was suprisingly small, really, and it wasn't long before he came into the infirmary. One bed was occupied, by a middle-aged man who had broken his leg after falling down a flight of steps while drunk, that very day. Clearly he had nothing to do with what Parker was searching for. He went into the side room and saw that the bed was neatly spread; but there was no sign of there ever having been an occupant.

Finally he went into the infirmary's small chapel and saw the sisters there, about twenty of them. They were all at their devotions, heads bowed and covered with their hoods.

'We have been praying,' said Sister Theresa, 'holding a service for another unfortunate death, a man killed in our own community.' Parker/Couhard turned without uttering a word and walked out through the side door of the infirmary.

'You think you're so clever,' he said to Sister Theresa, 'but I know she's been here, and you have sent her away. Where is she?' As he spoke the other members of the order came out from the chapel and congregated in the narrow passage behind Sister Theresa.

'Go in peace, Sheriff. I sense that you are a warlike man and that you are not good for this woman. She will come to you in her own good time.'

'You are obstructing the law. I could shoot you right now. Tell me where the woman is.' His fingers twitched above the gun in his holster.

'Shoot this grey head if you will, Sheriff, but that girl is not yours to take away.'

'We'll see,' said Parker, 'we'll see.' He turned on his well-shod heel and strode away.

It was only once the sound of his footsteps had died away that Sister Theresa turned to an apparent member of her order, one who was more slightly built than the others. The woman threw off her hood and looked palely at her friend, the woman who had nursed her so devotedly.

'My baby?' said Emily Quinn.

'Don't worry,' said Sister Theresa, 'I will go and see Katie-Jo in a few minutes. All will be well. You'll see.'

But her words rang hollow in her own ears.

Just the previous day Hank, the baby, had developed some kind of stomach infection. Gone was his normally placid temperament and, expelling matter from orifices at both ends, he had shrieked his protests loudly for half an hour at a time. Katie-Jo did not think this would be good for his mother, who had still not fully recovered, or for some elderly sisters, who needed their sleep, so she had taken the baby home with her.

Fortunately, during the early hours of the morning he had recovered from his attack of the croup and he had been feeding normally since. He had regained his usual good nature and was alternately patting her face and trying to pull her hair as she walked back to the mission. She had not yet heard the good news about the young woman, who, she was fairly certain, was this Emily of whom people had been speaking, but she had watched her making progress. Soon Hank would be with his natural mother.

For some reason this caused her to feel a pang of regret. At first she had resented having a baby imposed on her; now, after only a few short days, she was regretting having to let him go.

A big man wearing a star on his chest was striding down the main street. Nat Parker was not about to give up his attempt to find the woman and he was heading for the mayor's office. There he hoped to get official backing in his guise as Ben Couhard whom, he was fairly certain, the mayor had never met. It was a chance he was willing to take to get what he wanted.

That was when he encountered the woman who was also walking along the street. He saw the direction she was taking. Parker had never actually met Quinn's granddaughter, who had been brought up elsewhere for certain family reasons. The old man had spent time with her, but well away from prying eyes. Nor was Parker aware of how badly the woman had been injured; for all he knew she had merely taken a bump on the head. Parker had not been present when the manservant had prepared the coach in which Emily had fled from his clutches, but he was spot on with his surmise that the bright-eyed child in the approaching woman's arms was the one he was looking for. He stopped in front of the woman on the boardwalk.

'Say, ma'am, are you on your way to the mission?'

'I certainly am.'

'Well, that's fortunate. So this is the little feller I've been hearing about?' He patted Hank on the head, but the child pulled back and gave the stranger a stony look. 'Mother and child doing well?'

'Yes, thank you. So what brings you here, Sheriff. . . ?'

'Couhard. I'm here from Afton, looking for the mother and child involved in that terrible event from a few days before, and I guess I've found what I'm looking for. Say, would you mind coming with me and answering a few questions? It won't take long.'

'Well, that sounds all right to me.' Katie-Jo was in no particular hurry, and it was possible that the sheriff from the other town might be able to answer some of her questions, as well as the other way about. With a trust that was woefully misplaced she let him lead her to the edge of town, where his horse was tethered.

Suddenly he suddenly turned on her and raised his gun.

'Put the baby down.'

'Who are you?' she said, aghast at what she had done: trusting a complete stranger so much purely because he wore a star and had an air of authority.

'You'll find that out soon enough, missy. I sense that you'll be the bait I need – along with this little guy.' He dealt her a blow on the head that dropped her senseless to the ground. He gagged her with his bandanna and flung her across his broad cowboy saddle. He set Hank beside her and jumped up behind them. He pulled his cloak around to conceal Hank, who was protesting with piercing shrieks, and set off, riding for the place from which he would conduct his campaign.

There was too much at stake for him to think of giving up now.

When Sister Theresa went out on her own errand, it was perhaps by malign chance that she missed witnessing Katie-Jo's encounter with the strange sheriff by only a few minutes. If she had seen Katie-Jo talking to the cloaked stranger she could have warned her off; as it was Sister Theresa came back to the mission barely ten minutes after she had left, having seen nothing. Emily was waiting there, inside the building, her face pale as she looked at the elderly sister.

'Where is she? And where's my baby?'

'She was not at the schoolteacher's home,' said Sister Theresa, 'Miss Landers took your boy there because he was ill and she didn't want to disturb you. It looks as if she was on her way back here; at least that is what the other teacher said.'

'Then I know what's happened,' said Emily. 'He's got them – I don't even need to *know* – I can *feel* it here.' She pressed her chest just above her heart. 'He's got them, and I must look for my baby. I must do it, I must get out of here now and get to see him!'

Sister Theresa had never been a mother but she knew how powerful the instinct was, had seen it many times.

'You can't go,' she said. 'For a start, you don't

know where they are, and in any case you are not fit to do so.'

'Oh, I know what will happen.' The woman lifted her chin. 'He'll come back for me, and when he does I'll have no choice but to go because I want to save my baby. That's what he'll be expecting. Well, I'll see to it that when I get to him he'll get the biggest surprise of his life.'

'In what way?'

But Emily remained tight-lipped about her plans for the lying sheriff.

CHAPTER FIFTEEN

Flint stood up as straight as he could, considering his injury, and looked the sheriff in the eye.

'Ben, you're going to *arrest* us? Guess I heard you wrong. What are you arresting us for?'

'How about breaking and entering, house invasion, damage to property and even theft?' said Couhard implacably. 'You are a pair of miscreants. Not to mention murderers.'

'What do you mean: "murderers"?'

'I've been along this road a little whiles. I heard the shots going off in the mansion. You've murdered another two men in there.'

'Really? I wonder if you've got your facts right,' said Flint. 'Why not go and ask them if they've been murdered – once you've removed their gags, that is? As for this piece of cow plop,' he indicated the fallen Coyle with the toe of his boot, 'he decided he was going to end it for me, and my friend here shot him purely out of self-defence.'

'Are you going to come quietly? My deputies will

140

be here any minute.'

'Then I guess we've all got a chance, Ben. Unless you kill me to keep in cahoots with your paymaster, Parker, I ain't about to go anywhere but in the direction of Greenville. Your Parker is headed there and he's going to end the life of a young girl and a small child. Do you think that's right?'

'You can't prove that.'

'I'll tell you what I can't prove just yet, but that I'm certain of. There's a body buried at the back of this very place, down in the flowerbeds. I'm guessing it's been there for a few days, and I'm also guessing that if you dig it up it'll be the body of a certain shareholder and financier.'

Ben Couhard stared at the younger man; for the first time since the encounter had started there was an expression on his face that showed a certain dawning of understanding.

'That can't be the case; you went to see Mr Quinn the other day.'

'Did I? Or was there a certain old man brought in, possibly one of Parker's relatives, who play-acted as Quinn to fool all of us into thinking he was still alive?'

'How can I believe you?'

'Put the facts together for yourself. Quinn dies in some fashion just after a young woman arrives unexpectedly, bringing an infant with her, and she departs – with the infant – just as hastily. I think I have enough facts here to show that the young woman was connected real good to Quinn and that there's a reason Parker didn't want the world to know about Quinn's early death. Tell me, was there a groundskeeper attached to this mansion?'

'Be quiet! You're under arrest I tell you.' There were beads of sweat on Ben's brow.

'Was he a big man, grey hair at the sides and a baldy head?'

'He might have been.'

'Guess that's probably true. What if I told you that I saw that very man die before my eyes, after he was pumped full of bullets by Gal Beemis, the same Beemis, who right after I captured him was found with a knife in his heart? And all because Beemis was about to confess his sins and sing like a little birdie. Ben, what happened to you? I usta think you were a bit pompous, but still an upright kind of guy. How could you let it go this way?'

There was a moment's silence between them, as Flint looked directly into the eyes of a man who had been a brother sheriff, then Couhard lowered his gun.

'Get the hell out of here before I change my mind,' he said. On the ground, Coyle gave a loud groan. 'Shuddup, you piece of shit,' the sheriff told him, 'you'll get all the medical treatment you need.' He turned on his heel and strode towards the house.

Flint and Ty, suddenly freed, turned to the painful tasks of getting to their horses, unhitching them and riding out on the trail of the murderous Parker.

They were back in town in record time. The first

place they went to was the mission. They entered the main building, where they found a young woman, who was wearing a hood, and an angry Sister Theresa. The sister looked beyond Flint and straight at Ty.

'What's he doing with you? He was trying to get to Emily just the other day. He is an evil man in league with the other evil that has come to this benighted place.'

'You've got it wrong, Sister Theresa. Ty here has helped me more than anyone. Katie-Jo trusted him, and she was right.'

Sister Theresa was now looking at him with widened eyes.

'You're hurt, I can see it in you, and the side of your shirt. . . .' She did not need to continue because Flint sat down rather heavily on one of the wooden benches set along the whitewashed wall. Sister Theresa went to his side.

'I've got a job to do,' said Flint faintly.

That was when the story came out of what had happened earlier that day. It was as Flint had suspected: Parker was in the area because he had a bolthole near by, which was where he would have taken the young woman and child. Flint was surprised to find that Parker had been using Couhard's name but that too made sense when he thought about it. In the confusion that would follow from using a false identity a man with evil intentions could get away with just about anything. Parker had committed a federal crime, but at this stage he probabably wasn't too worried about that.

Ty had listened intently to what had been said, as did the young hooded lady who was also in the room.

'I'll get on to this,' said Flint, but it was clear that he was in some pain.

'You'll do what I tell you – right now,' Sister Theresa said, looking at him with a stern fondness that he had not known she felt for him. 'That wound badly needs attention.'

At the opposite end of the room the young woman threw off the hood that had concealed her pale features. She stared across the room at Ty, and that young man looked back at her, the colour draining from his own features. He came forward; she shrank away from him.

'Emily, it's me, I came back.'

This was her cue, for she slapped him so hard on the face that his head was rocked back on his shoulders. For a split second it looked as if he was about to return the blow. Ty had been in a few barroom brawls in his time and his instinct was to give as good as he got, but luckily he restrained himself in time. He looked at her with the astonishment of a man who has offered flowers to a woman only to have them flung down at his feet.

'What's wrong? I've been trying to see you since I heard the news about the woman and the coach. They wouldn't let me in.'

'Much good that would've done you, much good you've done,' said the woman. 'Because of you I had to go away from my family, what was left of it; I had to spend over a year away from all that I knew, just when at last I was getting to know Granddad. Then I came back and . . . all of this.'

She was not expressing herself clearly, the words were coming out in choking gasps. 'If I had been there all the time it could have been so different. Papa – my own papa – told everyone I was dead. That's how much shame you brought.'

'I swear I didn't know anything about this,' said Ty, 'I've been on the trail, and every time I came back to Greenville I looked for you. I swear that's true. I went to Afton too.'

'You didn't try hard enough, then.'

Ty looked at her helplessly.

While this confrontation was taking place Flint had left the room to get his wound washed and seen to by Sister Theresa, who seemed intent on using her energies to fuss over him. He soon had some padding made of cotton on his side, bound with a strip of linen. Below the cotton was some kind of liniment that burned like blazes.

'That hurts worse than the bullet,' said Flint mildly. 'Well, I'm going over to my office for a change of shirt. Thanks for your attentions, Sister Theresa, but I have a job to do.' Standing up he towered over her, but she surprised him by smiling.

'You're a stubborn man, Joe Flint.' She stood on tiptoe and kissed him on an unshaven cheek. He looked at her in mild astonishment.

'Ty, come with me,' said Flint as he headed out of

the building. 'Every second wasted here could make a difference.'

As he turned to go, moving into the light from the window, Emily noticed his shoulder, which had been partly concealed from her by the shadows in the room.

'Wait. What's wrong with you? There's blood.'

'This?' he said with a grimace. 'Nothing, just a flesh wound. Made by the folks who wanted to stop us finding out the truth about your grandfather.'

'My grandfather? But he's dead.'

'I don't rightly know the answer to that one yet,' said Ty. He turned to go after his new-found friend the sheriff.

'Wait,' said Emily.'Why are you doing this? You don't need to help Sheriff Flint. This isn't your fight.'

'It maybe wasn't a whiles ago, but then I heard what they tried to do to you, and they did this to me.' He indicated the wound on his shoulder. 'I guess this Parker feller needs to give me a few answers too.'

He flung out of the door and strode off to the sheriff's office.

Sister Theresa looked at the young woman. There was a look of understanding on her face.

'He'll be fine,' she said.

'What?' Emily flared up as she stared at the sister to whom she owed so much. 'Why should I care? He can get his fill of bullets if he wants.'

'There is nothing we can do but wait.'

Emily looked as if she was going to explode again,

her temper in tune with her red hair, but instead she forced herself to stay calm and look at the older woman.

'Do you have any weapons here at all?' she asked.

'Emily, what are you thinking? We do have a couple of guns, an old Colt and a rifle, because once or twice, out here in the frontier, we've had to defend ourselves.'

'Where do you keep them?'

Sister Theresa came forward and took Emily by the arm.

'My child, they are safely stored away in a trunk in my study, and that is where they are going to stay. You have not recovered yet from a serious illness; you cannot go out there after that wicked man.'

'It's my child.'

'I know. We will pray for his safe return; now come with me.'

'No, Sister, I want to go into my room and think about things.'

'Very well, you may leave.'

Sister Theresa kept a close watch on the young woman until she had gone into the room she had been granted earlier. Emily, walking slowly, made a good show of going in there, but she had a glitter in her eyes that said the matter had not ended yet.

On the ride up to the hills outside Greenville, as Flint steered his horse through a wide stream and through the thickets of trees that threatened to bar their way, he spoke briefly to Ty, who was riding beside him on his own steed.

'This Parker, he's as slippery as they come. He took Katie-Jo for a reason. I think that reason is simple enough to guess: he's trying to lure us up to see him.'

'What good would that do? And why would he do it on his own?'

'Don't you see? He never really thought that those clowns back there would hold us for long. He didn't figure Couhard was going to turn up, but he expected us to blast our way out of there and get back to Greenville eventually.'

'But why kidnap the woman?'

'It's his way of getting us to go there,' said Flint. 'Don't think he's going to let her go, by the way, because he's not that kind of man. He thinks she's Emily. He didn't know her real well and when he saw a woman going to the mission . . . I'm guessing he didn't question her too closely before he decided to take some action.'

'But she'll have told him by now.'

'And he won't believe her. He'll think she's lying just to protect herself and Hank. The truth is, he wants us good and dead and he won't let up until we are.'

'Then how do we get him?'

'That's what we'll have to decide.'

They dismounted, Flint from his roan and Ty from his mustang, at the foot of a hill that looked deceptively gentle and was heavily wooded with trees and bushes. They tethered their horses. Both men knew that their actions over the next few minutes could result in life or death for them both.

'I say we just rush at the cabin and go in, guns blazing; that way we take him out real fast.' Ty was not a strategist.

'That would work,' said Flint, 'but you're forgetting two things: the woman and the baby. That approach is real likely to take them out too, and that ain't the point.'

Ty fell silent, realizing that Flint had a good argument. The woodland around the cabin had been cleared, and it was obvious that this was a retreat that Parker had used before for whatever nefarious purposes. The pathway around the cleared area was well-marked out and it was easy to see how he would have been able to reach the building, which had windows at the front and side.

It was also clear that if they went in that direction they were courting death and might as well have painted targets on their chests. There was no sign of life from the building, but that could change in a moment.

Instead Flint went into an even more heavily forested part of the slope and began to climb. He paused once or twice and it was obvious that he was in some kind of physical distress, but he did not say a word to his companion. Ty was too keyed up by their present circumstances and what they were about to do to take much notice.

'You're going to act as the decoy,' said Flint. 'I want you to get over there and shout "Parker". If he makes the mistake of appearing at a window, shoot, but only if you're certain it's him.'

The young man was not lacking in bravery, as he showed when he came out at an angle towards the cabin, and sheltered behind a large pine tree, the dark scent of the needles cloying his nostrils.

'Give it up, Parker!' he yelled. He quickly showed himself in front of the tree: not his whole body, just his right side, then retreated just as quickly. Nothing happened. This gave him a false sense of confidence so he revealed his form for a moment longer. That was when the shot blasted out from the direction of the window, a shot that hit the bark of the tree and raised a shower of splinters. Ty was just barely able to get out of the way before he too would have been hit.

'Give it up, ya bastard!' yelled the young man, exerting his not inconsiderable lung-power. 'I'm coming in to get ya.' This time he was all fired up, the blood racing through his system, his instincts urging him to go forward and attack the cabin.

Flint slowly struggled up the hill through the bushes, moving with great caution because there was no doubt that the gunman in the cabin would be looking out for any sudden movements. Chances were that signs of any disturbance, even if made by small deer or a large rabbit, would draw his fire. Flint fervently prayed that he would not disturb any creatures that might bring that gunfire in his direction.

He found himself at the side of the cabin, facing on to the side window. He was in a rather odd situation here, because the ground sloped upward as he faced the window – a simple square of thin glass set in a wooden frame. Beside this window was the one area of land that had not been properly cleared, probably because Parker had never actually thought he was going to be involved in a shoot-out.

Like most of his ilk, Flint was wearing the trappings of a horseman. He had on gauntlets, reaching up the lower part of his arms, that he was due to remove if he was going to engage in gunplay. Around his neck was a bandanna, and he still wore his hat, wide-brimmed to shade him from the sun.

He was about to do something that he would never have considered in ordinary circumstances. But even as he crouched there in the bushes – during which time he heard Ty shouting at the gunman – Flint caught a glimpse of what was happening inside. Katie-Jo was slumped in an old chair set against the far wall. Beside her, on a table, looking puzzled, was Hank, his plump legs dangling over the edge. Crouched at the open front window was Parker, obviously ready to fire at any intruders. Flint felt a burst of energy fill him as he readied his body for the fight to come, his pain and fatigue dropping away for the time being.

Flint was not particularly fat, but he was solidly built. He took off his gauntlets, wrapped his bandanna around his face and tied it securely at the back. He replaced his hat and pulled it down low over his face, pulled his gloves on more firmly, and took a deep breath. Just as the gunman opened fire on his visibly approaching enemy, Flint jumped for the window with all his might, keeping his head low and smashing out with his fists.

There was a loud crash and the glass, which had not been designed to withstand such an attack, shattered into a myriad pieces as it exploded inwards, luckily most of them falling within a few feet of the frame so that the baby and the helpless woman were not injured.

The woman was roused enough from her stupor to emit a scream, while Hank, unaware of the gravity of the situation clapped his hands together and gave a loud cry of joy as if he was being given an evening's entertainment.

'You bastard!' shouted Parker, turning to face the intruder. He would have fired, but he had just loosed off many shots in the direction of the other attacker and he had not had time to focus on Flint.

'No you don't.' Even as he said the words Flint thumped downwards with his right fist on the gunman's shoulder and the weapon went flying out of Parker's grasp when his nerveless fingers let go. The men fought then, hand to hand. Parker quickly recovered the power to his arm because he was fit, fitter than Flint. As they fought it was obvious that he had been a boxer at some point on his life. This gave him the edge over Flint, who stumbled backwards, colliding with a chair that snapped apart as he fell heavily on top of it. He forced his body upwards but received an upper cut that sent him sprawling to to the ground amid the ruins of the chair, unconscious.

'Leave him alone!' screamed Katie-Jo. She tried to get up from her seat, but Parker had tied her wrists to the back with a length of strong twine earlier that day.

'Too late for that,' said Parker. He picked up his gun and fondled it rather lovingly. 'I'm doing what I should have done in the first place. You'll all be out of my way and I'll lean on Couhard so much that his eyes'll pop out of his fat face.'

Parker was just about to shoot Flint in the head when there sounded a loud thump at the door of the cabin. Ty had obviously come to the mistaken conclusion that Flint had succeeded in taking out their enemy.

'Don't do it!' screamed Katie-Jo.

The door swung open, but before he could raise and train his weapon Ty found himself confronted with his armed enemy. Parker did not hesitate: he shot the young man at point-blank range. Ty gave a groan as the bullet met its target and he fell away from the doorway. Katie-Jo screamed again and a smile of satisfaction came over Parker's smug features.

'You just keep screaming, because you'll be quiet enough soon, young lady, when I put a bullet through your brain – and his,' he added looking at the infant, whose face had crumpled. Hank was terrified now as he crawled off the table and landed heavily beside Katie-Jo. He clung to her legs and sobbed.

'You've served your purpose. Luckily there's a

ravine near by where I can get rid of everyone. But first, let's deal with this one.'

Parker was nothing if not a methodical man: he turned his attention to the sheriff lying on the ground. Flint showed signs of waking, but he was weak from loss of blood from his wound and the blows he had received earlier. He was not going to be able to defend any of them in time; he sat half-up just as Parker was training the gun on him.

'Goodbye, Sheriff Flint,' said Parker. Katie-Jo had stopped screaming, and the child too suddenly fell quiet.

'I wouldn't do that,' said a soft, almost childlike voice. Parker felt cold hard steel on the base of his neck. 'Drop the gun.'

He did as he was told and the pressure eased. He turned and found he was facing Emily, who had an antique weapon in her hand and a cold glitter in her eyes.

'So, you've arrived. I thought I was going to have to come and get you,' said Parker, his voice suddenly soft.

You could say what you wanted about the man, but even with the odds seemingly against him he still had a degree of aplomb such as many a person in a similiar situation would have lacked. 'That's not a proper gun,' he said, 'it's a trophy, a Colt 1848 pocket revolver. I doubt if it's been fired in more than ten years; you're more likely to blow your hand off with that thing than to drop me.'

'Want to try?' invited Emily.

'You know, I think I do,' said Parker.

All the time he had been speaking he had been getting closer to her. Suddenly he struck out like the snake he was, smacking her arm to one side. Her finger spasmed on the trigger, and the weapon, belying his assessment of it, gave a mighty roar. The bullet bypassed Parker and drove into the wooden floor, cracking apart the dry planks.

Parker grabbed at Emily's throat with the obvious intention of silencing her for good. He was a strong man and could have snapped her neck with ease. His black, glittering eyes stared deep into hers as he wrapped his strong fingers around her frail neck. Parker, she could see, was *enjoying* himself.

So concentrated was he on what he was doing that he failed to hear the faint crunch of glass being trodden behind him. The chair might have fallen apart when the heavy sheriff fell on top of it, but the loosened legs were solid enough – and so it proved when Flint, still swaying but rapidly recovering some of his old strength, brought one of them down with all his might on the back of Nat Parker's head.

CHAPTER SIXTEEN

Emily Quinn stood at the graveside in Cemetery Hill, Greenville's cemetery. She dropped a single sunflower on the grave, then stood there awhile. Her eyes seemed blurred but she had no tears. Flint stood respectfully a few feet away and waited until she was finished, falling in step beside her as she walked out of the cemetery.

'So who was he?' asked the sheriff as they walked into town. They were heading back to the mission that had been, for a short while, a huge part of her life.

'His name was Frank Sousa; he was half-Mexican.'

'What was his job?'

'He was a factotum and groundsman, the only person my grandfather ever really trusted.'

'So, what happened that day?'

'I guess you know I'd been sent away to a farm owned by grandfather to have the baby? He never intended to have me back – thought I'd disgraced the family name. He even told people I was dead, that I'd died in childbirth. He was really convincing.'

'Yes. I guess he must have been.'

'Even Parker bought his story. But that wasn't the way of it at all. Old Douglas secretly wanted to fund me and the baby to start all over again. He sent enough money for us to be supported for years, and he had a change of heart about seeing us.'

'Why?'

'I guess it's complicated.' Emily stared ahead; the scar on her forehead was still obvious. 'He started failing, really failing. It was his heart; he'd strained it in his early days and he knew, now, that his time was limited. He grew weaker and he wanted to see his grandson.

'Parker was waiting too – he'd found out the old man was due to meet his Maker. Once Douglas died, there was not a relative left to claim the estate, so it would all go to Parker and his clan.'

'Then you came along.'

'I turned up out of the blue, but only because Granddad had sent for me. The old man told Frank Sousa that I was to inherit everything. Grandpa didn't have long to go. But Frank got wind that Parker was after me, having learned I wasn't dead after all from that sneaky sister of his, and Frank prepared to take me away, to hide out of town.

'I was with Grandpa the day he died of heart failure; he'd left everything to us, and Frank mourned, but we had to run. I left the body of my grandfather all alone in that big, musty house. He didn't deserve that. He was the richest man in town

and he had nothing in the end, not even his life.'
The girl shed a single tear.

'That was when Beemis, who had already been
hired by Parker, tracked us down. He knew roughly
in which direction you were headed – Greenville
wasn't far away and it was a place you knew – you
knew where you could shelter.'

'That's right.'

'And that's when Beemis—'

'I don't want to talk about it. He's dead and
Parker's going to hang. For what he did to us all,
especially to poor Frank.'

'Then I came round, an interfering idiot in his
eyes, and Parker used his old, colluding uncle to fool
me into thinking Quinn was alive. While you were
still alive Quinn had to be too. Once you were out of
the way Parker could steamroller in and take everything.'

'I just can't stop thinking about Ty.'

'Neither can I, if it hadn't been for him – and you
– I would've been a goner.'

'It was my fault you were dragged into all this in
the first place.' They could both see in their heads
the terrible picture of Ty, lying face downwards at the
side of the cabin, a hole torn clean through him.

Sister Theresa was there to greet them as they arrived
at the mission. They could hear the sound of a child
gurgling with contentment inside the old infirmary.

'Come in,' she said. 'He's here, and so is Katie-Jo.'

They entered along with the old woman. Katie-Jo

was standing there holding Hank, who gurgled with delight when he saw them and kicked out his legs and waved his arms in an attempt to get, not to Flint this time, but to Emily.

A figure lay propped up on the bed. It was Ty, his upper torso heavily bandaged. He smiled and grimaced, one expression after the other as he strained his neck to look at them.

'Relax,' said Emily, 'you're in the best of hands now, isn't he, Joe?'

'He certainly is,' said Flint, nodding at Sister Theresa. 'You've got to thank Emily here for stopping the flow of blood, stanching your wound and waiting with you for two days until we could get you off that hill. I might have tried to move you sooner and then you'd've been a goner.'

'Thanks, Emily,' said Ty. He gave a groan of pain. 'Busted like this, I'll never work as a cowboy again.'

'That doesn't matter,' said Emily, 'we've got a big house to restore so we can bring up our kids.'

'Kids? You've more than one?'

'We will have.' She bent over and kissed him on the forehead while Flint took the weight of Hank, who tugged at his hair. 'And you've to be well enough to attend Granddad's real funeral in Afton, once all the legal matters have been sorted out.'

'I'm sure going to miss this little feller,' said Joe Flint, 'won't I, Hank?'

'You can come over at any time,' said Emily, 'and by the way, his name isn't Hank.'

'What is it?' asked Katie-Jo.

'Ty Junior,' said Emily, and her soon-to-be husband smiled despite his pain.

'Time we got out of here,' said Flint, 'to leave these two alone.'

Katie-Jo agreed, and once they had said their goodbyes to Sister Theresa and the child they now knew as Ty Junior, they strolled together down the main street as if they didn't have a care in the world.

'I don't know if I can do this,' said Katie-Jo.

'What?'

'Be with a man who is in danger all the time, or who brings danger down upon me.'

'There's no danger any more,' Flint pointed out.

'But there will be, Joe; there will be.' She turned and faced him. He was taller than she was by a good eight inches. He lifted her chin with his finger and searched her eyes with his.

'I can't promise there won't be any more of these affairs, but give me a few more years and I'll go into business. I'll leave this job behind and we'll settle down.'

'You promise?'

'I'll do my best.'

'Then that's good enough for me.'

Standing in the shadows of the boardwalk on a bright day he kissed her long and hard on willing lips. A few passers-by looked on in disapproval, or in the case of the men, envy.

The two lovers were quite oblivious to them.